The Women Who Forg[ot]
and Other[...]

Nisha Susan is a writer and editor. She grew up in India, Nigeria and Oman and lives in Bangalore. She is the co-founder of two award-winning media companies, The Ladies Finger and Grist Media. She currently writes 'Cheap Thrills', a column on millennials, time and obsessions, for *Mint Lounge*. She was formerly features editor, *Tehelka* magazine and also commissioning editor for Yahoo! Originals, a longform destination for Yahoo! India. Her non-fiction is focused on culture, gender and politics. Her fiction has been published by *n+1*, *Caravan*, Penguin, Zubaan and others, and often explores the intimacy and strangeness that the internet has brought to India.

Praise for *The Women Who Forgot to Invent Facebook and Other Stories*

'Calling the stories "millennial", though, is not saying much. What they do best is exhibit a generous and refreshing curiosity about the deceits and desires of life in the cities of post-liberalisation India.' – Amrita Dutta in *The Indian Express*

'Wicked, hilarious, sassy and the perfect antidote to lockdown blues ...' – Resh Susan in *Vogue*

'I was in for a surprise. In Nisha Susan's worlds ... you are indeed the protagonist, or their friend. You are the background noise, or the muse incarnate. Susan's acute observations of life mean you're seen.' – Pragati K.B. in *The Hindu*

'There's no doubt that women protagonists and female friendships steal the show in this collection ... English expands, heaves, sways and becomes a thing of local beauty in Susan's deft hands.' – Rashmi Patel in *Scroll.in*

'Her writing is funny and acutely self-aware as she lends nuance to the most mundane, everyday situations.' – Shikha Kumar in *Open*

'It is a riot and a half, because Susan steadfastly refuses to genuflect before the grand altar of political correctness, preferring to present her protagonists with their unsightly warts portrayed to maximum advantage.' – Anuja Chandramouli in *The New Indian Express*

'The language crackles to keep tempo with her characters' whimsies, quips abound and idiosyncrasies get their due idiom ...' – Sonali Majumdar in *Hindustan Times*

'The stories are stamped with Susan's unmistakable signature—the wry humour and keen observations that readers familiar with her writing will recognise immediately.' – Shreya Ila Anasuya in *Firstpost*

'The humour is distinctly mocking, but very effective at demolishing moth-eaten, but still-going-strong tropes.' – Sheila Kumar in *Deccan Herald*

'[A] clever, clever book ... Full of heart, terribly funny, and always surprising, this collection of short stories is about millennials butting heads with a world of predetermined destinies, aided by an air of hope and possibility ...' – Mathangi Krishnamurthy in *Biblio*

The Women Who Forgot to Invent Facebook and Other Stories

NISHA SUSAN

cntxt

First published by Context, an imprint of Westland Publications Private Limited, in 2020

Published by Context, an imprint of Westland Books, a division of Nasadiya Technologies Private Limited, in 2023

No. 269/2B, First Floor, 'Irai Arul', Vimalraj Street, Nethaji Nagar, Allappakkam Main Road, Maduravoyal, Chennai 600095

Westland, the Westland logo, Context and the Context logo are the trademarks of Nasadiya Technologies Private Limited, or its affiliates.

Copyright © Nisha Susan, 2020

Nisha Susan asserts the moral right to be identified as the author of this work.

ISBN: 9789395767637

10 9 8 7 6 5 4 3 2 1

This is a work of fiction. Names, characters, organisations, places, events and incidents are either products of the author's imagination or used fictitiously.

All rights reserved

Typeset by SÜRYA, New Delhi

Printed at Nutech Print Services-India

No part of this book may be reproduced, or stored in a retrieval system, or transmitted in any form or by any means, electronic, mechanical, photocopying, recording, or otherwise, without express written permission of the publisher.

'Lord, grant me chastity, but not yet.'

– St Augustine

Contents

The Women Who Forgot to Invent Facebook	1
The Trinity	10
Teresa	31
The Gentle Reader	53
No Filter	85
The Singer and the Prince	108
Missed Call	127
Workout of the Day	147
How Andrew Wylie Broke My Heart	170
The Triangle	190
Mindful	198
All Girls Together	205
Acknowledgements	219
Copyright Acknowledgements	221

The Women Who Forgot to Invent Facebook

I met Lavanya when I was nineteen and then everyone else in the world through her. When we left college, we still hung out a lot. It was 2001 and we drank a lot. We made friends with strangers. We left jobs after three days because we hated them. We carried small tubes of toothpaste in our rucksacks, brushed our teeth in the pub's narrow loo to scam our parents and drove on our spindly Lunas to our homes at opposite ends of the city.

One night, Lavanya's younger brother Akhil joined us at Vicky's. We were surprised to find him good company. Akhil was perfect. He was an insider, so we didn't have to behave ourselves. He knew which men we were into, which ones we had slept with, which ones we had considered. Akhil was enough of a social animal that he kept track of the goings and comings in Vicky's. He was enough of an outsider to our lovely twosome that we could use him as audience when we wanted to be outrageous, when we wanted to rehash old stories that only we laughed at. How Velu the pub owner never drank, but was in love with Ammini, the beautiful hard-drinking goddess who had been coming in night after night for years. How, when I was crushing on Jerry, I had managed to play it cool for weeks, only to lose it totally in the end. When I bumped into him outside the tiny loo, I looked up and mumbled: I've met your mother once.

Lavanya and I speculated that Akhil was gay. We even tried to set him up a couple of times, I think. One night, we made friends with an Australian boy, Darren, who was swarming with studs and had a Zapatista t-shirt. Akhil and Darren were all over each other. I have a hazy memory of standing outside Vicky's after Velu, the teetotaller pub owner, had personally escorted us out. Lavanya was looking for her bike keys and I was smoking. We had decided that Akhil would take Darren home because he was too drunk to go back to his PG. Akhil was giggling and leaning on Darren, who was taller by several feet. I saw Akhil trace Darren's nipples through his thin Zapatista t-shirt.

The next day Lavanya called me, alternately whooping with laughter and crying. She had sobered up on the dark way home, having lost Akhil and Darren several times for short worrying bursts. At home, she had let them in quietly without waking her parents and fallen into her bed.

In the morning, her mother and father were very severe after the chaste and sober Darren had left. The previous night, while the siblings slept, Darren had woken up, stripped and for some inexplicable reason walked out of Akhil's bedroom into the parents'. Hearing strange noises in their bathroom, the parents woke to the astonishing sight of a stark-naked white boy peeing lavishly into their commode.

Lavanya and Akhil and I went to Vicky's. And in the weeks that followed, Lavanya met someone. I met two someones. Akhil got laid. Darren got laid. Darren said he was bi. We introduced him to a boy we thought was gay. He wasn't, but his friend Somu was. Somu's friend George was seeing my friend Nayana. Nayana slept with Akhil, but only once. I stopped drinking.

We went to Vicky's. I met Tridip. We went to bad movies. He drove me to Yercaud. I bought him an expensive graphic novel. After three months, we still had not slept with each other. I got mad and slept with Darren, who was still bi. Somu cooled off. Darren left. He wrote from Australia. Tridip and I slept with each other. He told me about his girlfriend. Akhil stopped drinking.

We went to Vicky's. Akhil left early to study for the GREs. Lavanya and I drank slowly. It was hot and the beer tasted awful, but it was all we could afford. I read aloud a conversation between Gerald Durrell and his brother about ouzo and how it tasted like goat piss. It made us laugh and we began carrying books to Vicky's. Unlike us, the mysterious reading boy came alone and never looked up from his book. He drank slowly and had eyes only for his slow-blooming page. No one knew what he was reading each evening because the jacket never came into view.

We read and did crosswords and slowly it became November. Akhil was writing his applications and sending them off. Darren wrote saying he was thinking of coming again and might bring his boyfriend.

But when he did come, it was with a girl, a French girl. She spoke no English, Darren spoke no French but Akhil did, so he was the only one who talked to her. Lavanya and I watched and wondered. We did not ask but we wondered.

Tridip came back. He asked me whether I wanted to go to Coorg. Remember Yercaud? We would have fun again. What about his girlfriend? Ask him, said Lavanya, what about his girlfriend? I'm damned if I do, I said. We drove to Coorg. We came back. We stopped on the way back to look at pelicans. There were none yet, but in the moonlight, we kissed a lot. My mother saw my Hickey and was in a rage. She shouted at me all week, saying that my super-clean room was too dirty. I called Akhil to ask him about applications. I downloaded one and filled it half-heartedly and went to Vicky's.

The French girl and Somu frequently had intense conversations. Somu was still not talking to me. Not since I had slept with Darren. I sat at another table but strained to eavesdrop. They were talking about Vilas. Someone had slept with Vilas? I suffered while waiting for Lavanya, who was late that day. Anand came and sat at my table. I smiled a lot at him but kept messaging Lavanya under the table. Come, come, come quickly. This man is boring me when all I want to know is who fucked Vilas. Hot,

hot Vilas. I typed the message, smiled at Anand and sent it to him accidentally instead of Lavanya. He left in a confused rage. When Lavanya came, I told her and we laughed so much I was exhausted.

I drank. She drank. One night, she slept with Vilas. Hot, hot Vilas. Vilas died the next week on Kanakapura Road and she cried. I was sorry for a while, but then I thought, what the hell. I was not allowed to cry when Tridip went away to his girlfriend. But hot, hot Vilas had fallen off his bike and died. And Lavanya did not want to drink any more. Still we went to Vicky's. We smoked a lot. We pretended not to be interested in who the French girl was doing.

One day in January, after we had returned from Hampi and the stupid bead necklaces had already broken, Lavanya said: Bloody woman. Can't speak a word of English. What does she say to guys?

I looked up at her, then at the French girl at a far-off table full of boys and laughed. I ordered us a pitcher and pepper pork. The next day, Akhil came back, having sent off all his applications. He chatted up an art student called Shruti, who had come to Vicky's in an orange sari petticoat and strings of jasmine wound around two Princess Leia lumps on the sides of her stupid little head.

Darren came back from Vipassana full of metta for all of us. Anand forgave me for the bitchy SMS. He agreed that hot, hot Vilas's death was a loss. We told Darren that we would pay for his drinks if he made a move on Anand. But Darren was not drinking anymore. All we could make him do was to go to the mysterious reading boy and ask him what he was reading. By the time he came back to our table, he had forgotten the name of the book.

Velu was angry with his cousin Muthu. Velu's mother had made him give Muthu a job at Vicky's. Muthu liked playing football and had long hair. In his first week at Vicky's, he did not blink when we stole mugs. And sometimes a whole pitcher. Velu made him cut his hair. Muthu went out and got stars carved into the stubble on his scalp. Velu yelled at him.

We solved crosswords and were bored by Shruti in the sari petticoat. One day she told us that her year-end assignment, the big one, was going to be about death. Because she had lost a loved one. Hot, hot Vilas. Lavanya looked enraged. I looked at Akhil and was sure he was about to laugh. Lavanya looked at Akhil's face and she laughed. We all laughed. Shruti in the sari petticoat cried. Akhil comforted her for her loss and slept with her.

We solved crosswords and were bored. Lavanya drew faces and moustaches on everything. She almost drew them on my applications but I took them away. The Iranian boy came but we were still bored. He didn't find our jokes funny. He liked it when we both hit on him, though he'd do nothing about it. He was scared of policemen. He tried to make Velu go to the gym with him. We saw him making eyes at the French girl and we were fed up to the teeth.

Lavanya was silent and I asked her what she was up to. At first, she would not show me. Then she giggled.

She had written our names on a piece of paper and was drawing lines.

Send him away, she SMSed me. I sent the Iranian boy to get cigarettes.

She wrote names all over. Lavanya, me, Akhil, Somu, Darren, Iranian Boy, Ammini, French girl, Jerry, Shruti in the saree petticoat, George, Nayana, Anand, Hot-hot Vilas, Tridip, Velu, Muthu...

She drew lines from name to name. He had slept with her. She had slept with him. And him. These two? Are you sure? Oh, don't you remember? You never told me.

When the Iranian boy came back, we shooed him away. Oh god, who sends these imbeciles who can't speak English to India? Go back to the Revolution.

These two, I'm not sure. After the first year, they didn't have sex. Godpromise, four years they did not. How do I know why? I mean I know why. Shut up and join the dots.

In an hour, the sheet was dark and we could barely see our names under the mess of criss-crossing lines. We looked in awe at the sex map. It crossed the country. It crossed continents. Every continent except South America. Well, Mexico...but not really. The sex almost-atlas. Sex marks the spot.

We ordered a pitcher and giggled when we saw Velu, the teetotaller pub owner. Chaste Velu, who had held hands with Ammini, the unattainable hard-drinking goddess, once, in a Lido afternoon show. She was feeling generous, the afternoon before she got married to someone else. Chaste Velu would be so horrified to realise he was connected on the sex map to me or Lavanya or the Iranian boy.

George told us that Nayana was leaving for Korea to learn dance. What did they dance like in Korea? Then Akhil got into two universities but got no schols. Tridip came back from San Francisco. He asked me whether I wanted to see pelicans. Darren went back to Australia. The French girl learnt photography. We went to Vicky's.

Velu's cousin Muthu quit. A cute, hard-drinking girl who came to Vicky's every Thursday had got him a job in an event management company in Chennai. She liked his style, she said. Velu raged.

What we need is a website, said Lavanya.

For what, I asked.

For the sex map. Imagine how useful this would be if it was online?

How would it work, I wanted to know.

We would all sign up.

Who is we?

Everyone, said Lavanya.

Why would they?

It would be useful. When you met someone new, you could go look them up and find out if they were lying about being single. You could find previous girlfriends and see whether he had good taste or bad taste.

No one would sign up, I said. What a lot of work for nothing. What would all the liars or cheaters do? Have a red light against their name?

Yeah, maybe you're right, said Lavanya. Why would everyone sign up?

A man in a nehru topi rose from a table and began to hand out small mangoes. He was middle-aged and bearded, and had a strange fluting voice. He came to each table and pronounced his judgement before deciding to give us mangoes. I like you, I don't like you, no mangoes for you, more mangoes for you.

At the next table, the Iranian boy was competing with the French girl in making smoke circles. Akhil wandered past, snatched some of our pepper pork and smiled at us. Lavanya looked at him walking away and said, 'What will I do when he's dead?' I was astonished. She changed the subject, but badly. Akhil darted back to report that the mysterious reading boy was reading *The Celestine Prophecy*. We groaned together.

So what happens on everyone's map when someone is dead? Like hot, hot Vilas.

No one dies on the map, I decided. No one dies on the map, she agreed, and drew moustaches on the table.

The Trinity

When had I started carrying a white lace handkerchief? We used to call those kinds of girls Kerchief Kumaris. We used to have names for everyone. And everyone had names for us.

We were goddesses. Meena, Annie and Nayantara. Even our names were like heroine-names. Meena and Annie had known each other since they were five. I met them in seventh standard. Though we never said it aloud, we knew that three beauties had more power than two or one. Like the Hindu gods. Or all those pop groups. Like the Wilson Phillips. We liked the Wilson Phillips. We pretended to like the fat one, but heart of hearts we didn't.

In college, when the three of us walked in, I used to feel like we were in those campus film-like slow-motion scenes. Not like the fat twenty-five-year-old heroines in Malayalam campus films, but Hindi film heroines. We were already thin. We were already tall. We were thin and tall before anyone else was thin and tall. We had danced every day since we were toddlers and we had thighs like those sexy stone statues. If you were very, very strict, you could call me fat because of my butt, but even I had a very slim waist.

We had good sunglasses, not those big, ugly Gulf-return ones. We wore ghagras at weddings before anyone else did. We draped dupattas over our elbows casually even though our arms ached by the end of the day. We didn't sweat. You don't understand that, having grown up here in Bangalore. If you didn't sweat in Kerala's climate, God had blessed you.

I know the real reason we were goddesses is because we were dancers. We were award-winning dancers, crowd-rocking dancers. People knew us in the youth festival circuit as the three girls from St Agnes, not so-and-so dance teacher's student. We had dance teachers, but we did our own choreography. We had a category that we always won: the fusion dance. Before us, no one knew what that meant. They had started the category when we were in the twelfth standard. We knew immediately that the way it was meant to be done was not the way it was being done.

Before we came on the scene, people either had a fast version of a Hindi film song or a Tamizh film song. And then they had two groups on stage dressed in different clothes: one in Western outfits doing some rubbish steps and one in Indian costume doing some bad classical steps. Sometimes they had the same dancers alternating between Western and Indian sequences. It was just rubbish.

We discovered A.R. Rahman. That seems like a stupid thing to say. But really we did. We discovered his was the best music for our category. Annie's cousin Peter was the first DJ from Cochin. You may have heard of him because nowadays he plays in Bangalore also. His professional name is DJ Spacey. As a favour to Annie, he would mix our tracks for us. But mostly we didn't need to do anything to A.R. Rahman tracks. They inspired us easily. For songs like 'Vande Mataram', our choreography looked so natural that even people who hated the fusion category could not really complain. As classically trained dancers, we had flawless execution. We were able to do things that the untrained Western dancers could not. In any case, the Western dance category was dominated by boys. And unlike most of the ground-kissing, terrified Bharatanatyam dancers, we liked to dance for fun.

As teenagers, we had spent all our free time in my empty house. My parents are doctors, so there was less of the strict supervision that most of our classmates suffered. The constant where are you going, who are you going with, who is calling.

At fourteen, Annie, Meena and I knew the whole final dance routine in *Dirty Dancing* by heart. We practiced sexy dancing with a chair. We bought four-inch heels and learnt to dance in them, though we never wore them outside. By the time we were eighteen, we had finished with sexy dancing and danced once again just for fun. We were constantly copying dance steps from videos and from Hindi movies and trying to make them better. We loved Saroj Khan. We were excited for some time by a young choreographer called Farah Khan who had done amazing stuff in *Jo Jeeta Wohi Sikandar*. But mostly we loved Saroj Khan. Tamil and Telugu films in those days were hopeless with their robot aerobics dancing. And Malayalam films! You know no Malayali can dance.

Except us. In our first year at Agnes, we sailed into the dance team, so meticulous in our preparation that not even a half-blind selector would drop us. Once we began competing, we were inevitable. We won thirty gold medals in our three years at Agnes. We won all over Kerala, in Madras, in Bangalore and in Delhi.

At first, we travelled to local festivals in the college bus with every other cultural team and a couple of teachers, all insisting on playing antakshari badly the moment they got on the bus. After the first couple of competitions, we travelled without chaperones. Sometimes we even drove ourselves to the competitions, driving like mad little boys from Cochin to Thiruvananthapuram, discreetly racing past the chaperoned college bus full of kathakali, bharatanatyam, mohiniyattam, mime and mono-act participants.

Thiruvananthapuram was the big youth festival, the one where scandals broke out, goondas arrived sometimes, people cried, people died. Every year, the kala thilakam, the student who won the maximum points (and this was usually a dancer who had won points across a dozen solo events), enjoyed glory across the whole state. Her name was splashed in headlines the size of ladies' fingers. Many famous movie stars had been 'discovered' after they became kala thilakams. Many people competed in dance competitions to become movie stars.

I remember us entering the venue that first year, our first time in Thiruvananthapuram. We carried our huge bags backstage, looking so good doing it that no one made fun of us. Not even the comment-adi boys sitting atop the green, mossy walls who usually would have a million things to say—aye, porter, aye coolie, pavum camel, poor donkey—things we could imagine them saying to other girls who made the mistake of being weighed down by anything. They didn't say anything to us.

We were not interested in the kala thilakam scene, only in our category and in having fun. Thiruvananthapuram was a city so famous for its rudeness that, in my mother's generation, Cochin families would never marry into Thiruvananthapuram families. (My aunt was visiting someone in Thiruvananthapuram and went shopping in the vegetable market. She was picking up different vegetables, testing whether they were green, ripe, rotten. The vegetable seller told her, 'Put them down, you old hag. Those tomatoes are not your husband's balls for you to squeeze like that.')

We found a tame taxi driver who would drive us quietly from the dorm to the beach and back very early in the mornings. We walked around in tight jeans, pretending to be NRI Malayalis who did not understand Malayalam. With sunglasses on, we looked as much as we wanted at the Jalakanyaka's perfect naked body. On all other trips, our parents had never allowed us to look at the statue. Their cars would gain sudden speed and you would only see her thigh or giant concrete breast flying by.

Backstage that first year at the Thiruvananthapuram festival, we already frightened the other girls, their crazy judge-bribing mothers and their super-expensive dance teachers. The floors were slippery with foundation, what seemed like kilos of face powder and glitter. Every surface was covered with thick snakes of jasmine and sparkling clothes that made good 'show'. In one corner, we could see Rukmini-teacher from Palakkad reducing her favourite new student to tears. 'When you do that mudra, you are supposed to look like you are opening a small silver sindoor box, not your father's suitcase!'

We smiled a lot and even helped some people with their hair and costumes. We were relaxed, not sweating under the dramatic makeup we did for one another. After the makeup was done, of course, we could not smile anymore. We sat blinking calmly, the broad coloured tails we drew at the edge of our eyes making us look like strange birds. We draped and pinned shawls over our costumes so that no one would see them until the very last minute.

We had decided that, along with our modern choreography, we needed a completely new look for Thiruvananthapuram. After much experimentation, we decided to combine sleeveless saree blouses and salwar bottoms with dupattas draped tightly over the blouses.

It had to draw attention to our perfect curves but not in some cheap cabaret dancer way. The first time in Thiruvananthapuram we knew we were taking a risk, but we were sure we could carry it off. We knew that, more than anything else, what would shock the public were our bare arms. Malayalis have this strange thing about 'sleeveless'. Sleeveless means bad girl. Usha Uthup-voice bad girl. Never mind that stomach and back and breasts are showing when you wear a regular saree blouse.

We were used to designing our everyday clothes and our tailors were our slaves. In return, they happily stole our patterns for their less imaginative clients. They wouldn't ever try to touch us sleazily or suggest that our necklines were too fast. But, for these new dance costumes, we had had to find a brand-new tailor.

The only man to go to was Blouse Mohan. Blouse Mohan never spoke, never chatted with clients. He never measured. Every woman in Cochin with the courage (which a surprising number had) went to him. You stood before him. Took off your dupatta if you were wearing one, moved your pallu aside if you were wearing a saree. You stood before him while he looked at your chest. When he was done, he looked at his notebook, wrote indecipherable things and never looked at you again. Meanwhile, you explained (to the top of his head) the occasion, the style, the look you were trying for. You were never sure whether he heard you. One of his dozen assistants would then give you a date to come and pick up your blouse. And on that day you would get the best-fitting, most flattering blouse you had ever had in your life. Courage was involved not just in letting a strange tailor stare at your breasts. It also lay in the possibility that Blouse Mohan might refuse to stitch your blouse. Oh, the assistant would tell you that saar was busy. But you'd know that you had been checked out and found wanting.

When we went to him, we stood quietly before him. We explained our requirements in detail, one professional to another, handed over our material, sure we would not be refused. Not even Blouse Mohan would dare refuse us. And it was true, the incredible costumes that we wore in Thiruvananthapuram and after, in those three years that we won thirty gold medals, the costumes that people raised eyebrows at, were all made by Blouse Mohan.

Our costumes became legendary. In the final year, when we went back to Thiruvananthapuram, the boys from SDA College did a bad skit that they called the St Agnes Kumaris Dance Drama. Three of the boys wore saree blouses and jumped about on the stage, their hairy stomachs bouncing above tight salwar bottoms. One of them wore a bra over his salwar bottom and pranced around, speaking in a fake aash-posh-Malayali-girl voice. Annie and Meena said it was annoying, but I was secretly thrilled that they had sat and planned a skit to make fun of us.

That first year, I remember Rukmini-teacher scolding her second favourite student. 'Beckon gently to Lord Krishna with your eyes, don't frighten him away with your ugly face!'

A few seconds before we went on stage, we did our secret ritual. We crossed our hands at the wrists, held one another's hands tightly, formed a triangle, leant back, and spun round and round. At high speed, in that tight space, beyond the duststorm of face powder our feet was creating, we could see the shocked dancers, teachers and mothers. But we didn't care. We were enjoying the rush and their shock. We stopped, dizzily dropped our shawls, ignored the gasps and went on stage.

Nobody had seen anything quite like us before. Even our friends from Agnes stared at the costumes and then forgot the costumes during our performance. I think I can still do that dance. I remember all our steps. It was a long performance. Eleven minutes of blood-rushing perfection that ended in our trimurti pose.

After Thiruvananthapuram that first year, everything was easy. Wherever we went, boys lined up to be helpful. To fetch, to carry, to have a quick, sneaky coffee between Western and fusion. We looked them in the eyes and laughed at their jokes as loudly as you can ever imagine classical dancers laughing. They went away saying we were 'frank' girls—a compliment they usually give to ugly girls.

It was at IIT Madras, towards the end of our first year, that we found our serious devotees. Staying at the IIT women's hostel, we were horrified by how little the girls maintained themselves. They had moustaches and they were reading all the time. Even during the festival, they were walking around sluggishly in nighties.

We, on the other hand, were on fire. From the moment we got off the bus, boys followed us around, offering to show us the beach, take us shopping, take us to Landmark, to Shakes and Creams, to Mahabalipuram, to see the famous IIT deer that ate Chinese food, to the best coffee on campus. Used to some degree of primness around wolfish Malayali men, we were liberated by the polite gratitude of IIT boys, who seemed like they had never been around women. They were smart but didn't assume we were stupid. They were funny but did not make fun of us.

At IIT, with five different contests over four days, we had a lot of work to do. For the first time, we had competition. The Madras and Bangalore colleges were quite good. We practised for hours, going over every detail. The rest of the time, we tried to figure out our lighting and sound systems with the volunteers. By the fourth day, even we were tired. Rehearsals, performances, after-performance flirtations, staying up all night on the lawns pretending to like Pink Floyd, we were ready to drop. Still we danced. We went to a disco for the first time that night and danced some more. The sexy moves had been in storage but not forgotten.

Past midnight, our taxi left us at the IIT entrance and we walked slowly, a dozen boys and three girls dragging our feet on the long road to the girls' hostel. I looked around at the boys and thought for the first time that I would like to kiss someone. At least four of the boys seemed like possibilities. These and other thoughts took us to the point where we decided, almost simultaneously, that we could not possibly walk another step. Annie, Meena and I lay down on that smooth road. The boys stood above us laughing quietly, trying to talk us into getting up, considering lying down on that road themselves. I am not the romantic type, but I remember the stars and trees and the boys' heads looming above us as if it was a photograph. At some point, a motorcycle drove past us, around us, and I saw a familiar face looking back in horror. It was Rukmini-teacher's favourite student, the one who in Thiruvananthapuram had opened the silver sindoor box like a suitcase. She was riding sideways on an IIT boy's motorbike. In a while, we got up gracefully, as if we had been practising all our lives to raise ourselves off a warm road in front of an audience.

Then two boys picked me up, balancing me on their shoulders. Annie and Meena were picked up too. We looked at each other, above the heads of the boys. We were laughing but we were not really. They carried us all the way to the hostel gate, where they stood waiting for us to disappear out of sight. A few hours later, when we surfaced to leave Madras, they were standing there, almost as if they had never left. At the bus stop they waved and I know at least one boy cried.

Never particularly talkative, we were silent on the way home. When we were back in college it was as if we radiated light, people were so careful and respectful around us.

So many things were unspoken between us that I can't tell you why I thought the three of us would have brilliant lives. We were beautiful, we were well-heeled, we were excellent students. I knew we deserved wonderful lives, more than our parents had, with their flab and sugar and high blood pressure.

When the three of us were still in school, our cousins who lived abroad seemed to have those wonderful lives. They and their husbands were trim, their Malayalam lightly accented, their family photographs gorgeously candid. One Christmas, we sat in a quiet corner of Annie's crowded drawing room, listening to the young male visitors talk. Brothers-in-law, cousins' husbands, cousins—they were all in their thirties and globe-trotting successes. At some point, the conversation turned to their wives packing their suitcases.

'I was in Dubai for three days and I realised that Sharon had not packed a single pair of black formal shoes for me. Throughout the conference, I kept hoping that no one would notice I was wearing black track shoes with my suit.'

'That's nothing, last month when I went to London, Mary did not pack any underwear!'

'That must have been intentional.'

Muffled laughter.

After dinner, we heard a voice raised in anger in the corridor. 'Six years I have been married to you and I packed your suitcase wrong once! Once! And you insist on telling everyone and shaming me.'

When I was thirteen, I read my first Mills & Boon. It was the first time that I enjoyed a book. Brought up on school-syllabus reading and my parents' musty collection, I was astonished to find books where people's clothes and the colour of the hero's eyes were described in every scene. I lent Annie and Meena the book and they loved it as well. After that, we smuggled romances into our houses and read them secretly; in each house, censure of the red-blue-green books was different only in degree. To the first dozen M&Bs I read, my real response was, 'Where are these people's parents?' They never seemed to have anyone bothering them. Later, I think, I forgot about that.

By the time we hit college, we no longer liked to read the romances in which the guy was experienced and the girl was a virgin. First we laughed at them, then we were annoyed by them. We did not like naïve girls. Towards the end of our first year, a couple of weeks after we had come back from IIT, a scandal rocked St Agnes, making it to the front pages in Kerala. Some of the hostellers had decided to have a pyjama party, and for some idiotic reason had stripped to their underwear and taken pictures of each other. As if this were not stupid enough, they had actually taken the roll to be developed at a photo studio in Cochin!

Flash! It was all over the tabloids and even all the big newspapers. It went online as well. Agnes threw the girls out. The girls were sent by their parents to colleges out of state. We didn't even laugh, their stupidity was so pitiable. Think of how careful we were.

Several boys from IIT had written to us. A few emailed us, even offering to take trains down from Chennai to see us, but we discouraged them. To be spotted in a restaurant with strange men was too dangerous. Later on, we figured that even in Cochin there were places we were guaranteed never to see someone we knew.

But back then, we were content to chat up boys on the Internet. We each wrote to several boys. Mails went back and forth ten times a day. The IIT boys had their own comfortable twenty-four-hour computer labs and no one to bother them. We had a harder time until Annie persuaded her father to get a dial-up connection. Every time the modem came on, making its distinctive, creaking, noisy tune, I wished there was some way of muffling the sound. As annoying as it was, it was still miraculous. It was the best thing to happen in our lives after cordless phones.

Over the next year, our social lives were planned carefully on the internet so that no one in Cochin suspected a thing. We arranged to meet boys on our out-of-town competitions. We each had fairly serious relationships, romanced boys in different small-town colleges, had sex with them in more anonymous big towns. We were together and strong and happy.

Then college was over. No matter how long I had awaited the end, it still felt sudden. I was admitted to the microbiology master's programme in Cochin. Meena and Annie had not applied anywhere, I found to my astonishment. Before I could figure out what was going on, my parents hustled me on a trip to Malaysia to visit my older sister.

When I came back two months later, I was fat. I had never been fat in my life, but two months of not dancing and eating really well had killed me. I pinched my waist and did not understand whether flesh was actually meant to feel that way. Repulsed by myself, I delayed calling the others. And strangely they didn't call me either.

My mother remarked that Annie's engagement seemed sudden. I nearly dropped the iron on my foot. Only the shame of being left out prevented me from running to the phone right then.

As soon as my mother was out of hearing, I called Annie. I pretended to be calm. 'What is this vishesham that I hear, Madam?' I faked a teasing tone.

Annie laughed. 'Isn't it wonderful? Who did you hear from?'

From my mother, you bitch, I wanted to yell. But I didn't. So I heard how Annie had met Rohan, an ophthalmologist her parents had found for her. The wedding was a year away, the engagement in a month's time. I sat down hard. What had happened to that sweet Telugu civil engineer she had been seeing for six months? Big-eyed, tall, warm, he and Annie had made a stunning couple. Just before I left for Malaysia, he had come to Cochin, defying Annie's orders, because he was going away to the US. I had driven Annie to the jetty and waved them off on their ferry ride. Annie had been in her NRI tourist disguise with a hat, sunglasses and fresh toddy in water bottles.

Now, in this phone conversation, I could not even ask about him. I knew the rules had suddenly changed.

While I scrambled to catch up, Annie told me to pack and be ready the next weekend. Her Rohan had paid for a five-day holiday at a local spa for the three of us.

I longed to call Meena but was terrified to. The next weekend, when I met them at the spa, ten kilometres outside of town, I knew I had been right to be scared. They did not remark on my appearance. That was frightening in itself. Annie spoke continuously of Rohan. I looked at his photograph and was astonished afresh. He was plain, acne-scarred and tubby. He had a sweet smile, but that was all that could be said for him. Annie said that they wrote to each other every day. In his latest mail, he had said that he was sending her a gold credit card.

Meena made jokes about Annie as if this were a romance. I wanted to hit her. When we actually had romances, we had never teased each other in that giggly, annoying Malayali-dubbed voice-heroine way. Why now over this whale in a white shirt? But I choked on the words.

It was called a spa, but it was actually a very strict naturopathy clinic run by Catholic nuns. I thought sourly that Rohan probably did not have to pay much for these military-bunker surroundings. For the next five days, we were woken up at dawn, given cucumber juice and led to yoga class. I kept falling asleep mid-asana and the others laughed at me. It was almost like being together again, but not quite. We ate sliced cucumbers, drank bitter-gourd juice at lunch time and had fruit for dinner at 7 p.m. The others fell asleep looking like angels and I glared at the ceiling, uncomfortable on the hard bed.

Between one massage and the next, I managed to get Meena alone. I tried to ask her casually about Annie's abandoned Telugu boy. Meena was infuriatingly uninterested.

A day later, while sitting in the sun with thick, smelly kuzhambu all over my body, I asked Meena about her own current boyfriend, a sweet Malayali boy at IIM Kozhikode.

'Mummy said no,' she said calmly.

'Your mother! Your mother said no?' I could not understand it.

Meena's mother was the most open-minded of all our parents. She had even agreed that Meena's elder sister in Bangalore could marry her Bihari boyfriend in a couple of years.

'But Keshav is a Bihari!' I said.

Annie and Meena looked at each other. Meena smiled, 'I know, I said the same thing to my parents. But Mummy says that Bihar is so far away, no one knows what a Bihari is really like. But everyone knows Latin Catholics were all originally fishermen converts. They drink a lot.' And that was the end of sweet Stephen.

We were having the special massage on the fourth day. I was incredibly sick of the spinach thoran and cucumber juice that I knew was coming. Even thinking of it was making me retch.

Three days of near-starvation had made no difference to my fat. The other two sat nearby, glowing, feet crossed elegantly at the ankles, murmuring to each other. Even the grumpy massage girls remarked on how beautiful they looked.

I suddenly caught what they were saying. Meena was saying to Annie. 'Mummy was joking that since Chechi's is a love marriage to a Bihari, they would not have to give dowry. But it's only a joke, ketto? It is a matter of our pride after all. They will give Keshav as much as they give my groom. Not as much as you, but at least twenty-five.' Annie nodded gravely.

I was shocked. Dowry! Twenty-five lakhs! Who were these women? Where were my friends? The rough hands scraping my back silently pushed down harder. The smell of the kuzhambu made me nauseous.

On the last morning, we sat quietly, combing our hair before the steam baths. I looked at my feet, which were usually smooth as a baby's bottom. Walking around the nasty spa's concrete courtyard with all kind of oils had given them cracks. While pretending to focus on my feet, I started a conversation with the others, deliberately turning to nostalgia. They resisted. I tried to get them talking about the future and the marriages they had in mind. Conversation flowed easily. I relaxed, too.

It must have been on my mind—I certainly had not planned to ask, but I blurted out, 'Will you tell your husband about your boyfriends?' Annie smiled, 'Perhaps, later.' Meena said no. Annie added, 'What is there to say anyway?'

I thought of Stephen always remembering to order Thums Up, not Pepsi or Coke, for Meena when we ate Chinese.

I thought of seeing Annie across a darkened hall in Delhi, tossing her long hair back, fully dressed from the waist upwards, astride her awed engineer, rocking her hips lightly, with concentration. I had watched till I fell asleep.

What was there to say anyway? I looked at them straight in the eyes for the first time since I had come back. 'Will you tell your husbands that you have had sex before?'

Annie and Meena looked at each other, a gesture I was growing to hate.

Meena said, 'But we haven't.'

Annie nodded. 'Never.'

I thought I was going to be sick.

The next day, the ride back was quiet, almost normal, devoid of the strange wedding chatter of the last five days.

At home, my father was patronising. A bad sign. Even he was afraid of us when we had been together, hiding from a force beyond his control by watching the news continuously. Now he patted my head and said, 'Depressed because your friend is getting married before you? Your turn will come too!' I wanted to kill him.

When classes started, it was a relief. I had a lot of work to do and did not want to think too much about the others. They had signed up for desultory courses, courses we all knew girls took only to abandon midway for an H4 visa.

No one knew me now. It was shocking. For the first time ever, I was victim to the comment-adi boys. As if they knew I was defenceless. I came home crying a couple of times. Then my father started sending a car and driver to pick me up. I, who knew that the car and driver was a leash you could never drop, thanked him for it. My boy with the magical eyes had lost interest and stopped driving up from Thiruvananthapuram. I could not remember the last time I had danced.

Two years later, I married Pradeep, who was midway through his MD in Bangalore. He did not listen to Pink Floyd. He did not surf the net. The only thing he had to say was that he spent his spare time playing badminton and TT. He had never had a girlfriend. After we got married, I knew that he had not been lying.

The day I got married, I stood for hours meeting hundreds of guests in four-inch heels, knowing it was the last time in my life I would be the centre of attention.

When I first moved to Bangalore, I met a mean woman during a bride visit. She told me that everyone would think I was what the Kannadigas call a halli-guggu—a country bumpkin—because of the handkerchief I held in my left hand. 'If you twist it any harder, it will disappear,' she said. I was so angry I swore I would never speak to her again. Only much later, years later, did I wonder when exactly I had started carrying one.

Recently, Pradeep's friends took us to see Saroj Khan's troupe perform at Bangalore Habba. After the show, Pradeep made fun of me, saying that I was regretting missing my chance to be part of the troupe. I also laughed. He told his friends that I had been a kala thilakam. The girl who had actually been kala thilakam in my second year had become a movie star. She was going to save Malayalam cinema from its eternal shortage of heroines. She was a powerful presence in three movies, all flashing wit and diamond nose stud. Then she married a fool comedian. He said he did not want her to act any more. She was never seen on screen again. I don't think I hate anyone as much as I hate him.

Teresa

*Ought to blow up my computer
but instead...
I google you.*
— Neil Gaiman

Last night I dreamt of Teresa again.
My dreams are realistic. When I'm worried about money, I dream about money. When I need to pee, I dream of going to the bathroom. Teresa. Who will tell me why I dream of Teresa?

I've only seen her alive for a few minutes. Never told anyone that I have.

Across the street I saw her, beautiful Teresa. I recognised her from Ajay's parents' photo frames. I stepped off the dirty beach at Juhu Chowpatty, with wet and sandy feet, and saw her.

I've slouched my five feet eight inches all my life, but there was Teresa—nearly six feet tall and coming out of that pasta place, striding like a movie star. Three men were following her in formation, like extras, all their heads turned towards her. They were laughing as she pretended to hitch up her plain black sari. She lifted her clouds of curls into a twist. She twirled a big, imaginary moustache like a child in an Annual Day folk dance. They laughed and I stared.

At work, the day after I saw Teresa, I was unhappy. Nothing seemed right. All week I was listless. The next week, my boyfriend, the only one I've ever had, broke up with me. He didn't make eye contact much, but when he did, he seemed angry. He seemed angrier when he realised I wasn't going to ask for an explanation. I already knew how lonely I was going to be.

'I am tired,' I typed into Google. The first link led to an empty, white web page. My heart slowed down as I glimpsed the single line of text on the page. At the very bottom, tiny letters asked, 'Tired? Tell us why.' That was all.

A few days later, Teresa drowned in a swimming pool. It was in all the papers and in all the blogs of many people who had never written about death before and were struggling to find eloquent words for it. For her. Teresa had a very popular design blog that a friend in America took over in her memory. Hundreds of people sent art, writing and memories to the blog, tributes to their friend Teresa.

Four years later, I met Ajay. I was twenty-nine, working in a bank's IT department and beginning to find lunch conversations physically painful when they inevitably turned to my twenty-four-year-old colleagues' wedding plans.

Though Ajay and I had both lived in Bombay for years, we met in Kerala. He was visiting his son Vinu. His parents had been taking care of Vinu since Teresa died. I was visiting my parents' best friends, who lived next door to Ajay's family. They were the closest thing to parents that I had. After a lifetime in the Gulf, they had moved to Ranni, and I visited them as often as I could without getting on their nerves.

Ranni was somehow both jungle-green and cement grey, and I hated it. But it had become my fake hometown after my parents died. I was sent to boarding school in Kottayam when I was six, seeing my parents for a couple of months every year in the summer when they came home from Qatar. When I was fifteen, they came home without warning and hung themselves in their Cochin flat. They didn't leave a note. My parents' friends took turns to be my local guardians, to help me finish school and get into engineering college in Bombay. Years later, it occurred to me that perhaps my father and mother had had AIDS. I had heard about other families in Kerala who had been deported from the Gulf because of it. And then I understood the hints from people in Ranni who had thought it important to let me know. Just in case I hadn't wondered why my parents had left me behind.

Ajay's parents lived next door. Next door meant up the slope in our hilly neighbourhood. His father had been a jet-setting minor diplomat in his day, but when they retired, his parents had decided to come back to Ranni. I had heard a lot about Ajay and Teresa from them but had never met either. Everyone still talked about Teresa in Ranni. They talked about how fair she was, her figure, how 'bold' she was, how 'simple' she was. When I was in Ranni, I tried to hide behind electric poles and trees. Teresa had driven around on a scooter, never tried to speak a word of Malayalam, hung out with the rubber tappers, and left each time with gifts of new saris and old furniture. Ajay was the youngest ever editor-in-chief of any Bombay newspaper, but Teresa had obviously been the more glamorous one to folks in Ranni. Except to Vinu, perhaps. But that was because she had died when he was barely a year old and he did not remember his mother.

All Vinu knew were his placid grandparents from whom he had learnt his elaborate, old-fashioned Malayalam. And he knew his father who appeared in Ranni once a month from Bombay. Was Ajay glamorous to Vinu? I never thought so. At five, Vinu preferred people like me, people who were dazzled by the unspooling of his small-boy thoughts in his old-man language.

That summer I watched him playing in the deep, rocky, rain-drenched lane beside the house with a child his age. After half an hour, the other child began crying in irritation. Vinu never understood why, but we who were watching were sympathetic to his playmate. Vinu was incapable of saying, 'Put the ball down.' He would say, 'Kindly deposit the toy.' He tried to distract other children from his hopeless lack of athleticism and his long, flailing skinny limbs with his flights of verbosity. 'I told my grandmother I don't want to bathe under a raincloud anymore,' he said to me. He meant he didn't like the shower, I think. I didn't ask. Vinu liked me because, like his grandparents, I did not interrupt his long monologues. In any case, I wasn't much of a talker. An exception in Ranni, where everyone was full of long, wild, gossipy anecdotes.

It was the first time that Ajay and I were both in Ranni at the same time. From the kitchen door, where I sat drinking tea one afternoon, I saw Vinu walking down the slope, loosey-goosey, hanging on to his father's hand. I remember feeling surprised at how small and wiry Ajay was. At how handsome his face was. Women loved him, I knew this instinctively.

That fortnight, I saw the hard, middle-aged women in the neighbourhood squeeze his arm, pat his head and feed him. Around him I saw them sinking into dreamy silences. Later, I learnt that things were no different in Bombay. I am sure women loved him before Teresa died, but now there was the added lustre of his tragedy.

I'd have liked Ajay just for not asking me stupid questions. It was disorienting to have someone from Bombay appear in Ranni. It was as if a time-traveller had arrived from the future. I could see everyone around us suddenly pretending to be blasé—about my height, my silence, my unmarried status—to match Ajay's cool standards. They were unnaturally tactful about the little friendship that developed between Ajay and me that holiday. After all, he was the small widower with a five-year-old liability. And I was the orphan giant.

After my break, when I was back in Bombay, Ajay called and asked me home to lunch. Not at whichever was the most fashionable new café, a choice I understood soon. We met at his beautiful Bandra apartment, the interiors of which I had seen in more than one magazine when Teresa was alive. Ajay chatted. About his occasional TV appearances, I think, and the impossible acrobatics of trying to sound intelligent on them. About Vinu. About his continued astonishment that his parents wanted to live in Ranni. The Bihari cook looked grim. I looked around.

In one corner of the living room, crooked on the ceiling, was a burnished replica of a big beehive made of hundreds and hundreds of tiny bells from dancers' anklets. I stared at it through the afternoon. A few months later, when we were married, I continued to discover strange and beautiful things around the house. When I opened the drawers of the bed with the extra sheets and pillows, I found the smooth, wooden insides covered in Japanese cartoons of a pink-haired boy having sex with a tigress with long eyelashes.

It was difficult to learn to bathe in the house. The shower cubicle with its walls covered with fragments of mirrors made me bigger, smaller, curved me, untangled me.

Ajay and I had sex for the first time after we were married. We were on holiday in Arunachal Pradesh. I felt like I was a puzzled eye in the ceiling watching as this man and woman contorted themselves into strange positions. Why was his mouth here, her leg there? I had felt the same eye-in-the-sky feelings with my boyfriend the few times we'd had sex, so it didn't surprise me. I learnt fairly quickly what Ajay liked. That part of our lives was taken care of.

Other things were simultaneously more easy and more difficult. Ajay's parents were wonderful. They insisted Vinu finish the school year with them. Ajay's mother told me secretly they wanted us—the newlyweds—to have some time alone before becoming parents together. 'It's not like Ajay is so familiar with looking after Vinu either. So, the burden will be on you. And that's unfair.'

Ajay's Bihari cook Mansoor decided to stop being grim. Instead, he told me, wiping what I could see were fake tears, that he missed Teresa bhabhi so much. She used to drink with him in the kitchen on Sunday evenings when Ajay bhaiya was not there. I never doubted that Teresa would have drunk with her cook, but the idea that she had ever stayed at home on a Sunday evening I found hard to believe.

I had read about Ajay and Teresa's life in the papers and now I could see it for myself.

Within two days of returning from our mini-honeymoon, Ajay's social life was in full swing. Whenever he was done with work, whatever time it was, he would come home to shower and change for the night. The phone would beep with messages every few seconds. By the time he came out of the shower, plans would have been radically changed. Where the original plan involved meeting one friend in town for a drink, now the evening would begin in town for a drink and then another in Phoenix Mills, then another for a last drink in Bandra and then to pop in at someone's party round the corner from Zenzi. Old Zenzi. No, new Zenzi. Nahin, yaar, old Zenzi.

Ajay drank well. Like he did everything else. He'd go from bar to bar, seem absolutely sober till 5 a.m., ferry us all some place for breakfast and fall asleep in the cab holding my hand on the way home. He'd wake a few hours later, bathe and be ready to work.

I was free to join any or all of these. It terrified me, the choices and the people. The first few times I was exclaimed over and hugged and smiled at and spoken to sweetly—I thought I would survive. But a few months after we married, Subbu arrived.

We were sitting in a bar in town around midnight. Ajay was having some argument about Kashmir with three other women when Subbu entered. Small and chubby, with the longest eyelashes I've ever seen. Subbu was an artist and had been away in Germany for six months. She had missed our wedding. Ajay and she had known each other since Valley School, and when she arrived it was as if the social jigsaw puzzle was complete. I heard the click.

From then on, all conversations around me seemed to go like this.

— I can't believe you don't remember *Jackie Brown*.

— I'm sorry, man. I was smashed when I watched it.

— You were not smashed. You hated it and you just don't want to say you hate a Tarantino movie.

— Shut up, Django.

— I'm telling you, his brother drowned in the school lake when we were about thirteen. How can you not remember? His brother drowned five days after he joined school.

— You guys have to stop making fun of her writing. She'll win the Booker and we'll all be up shit creek. All those people who made fun of Mary Roy's crazy daughter who hung about Kottayam with her laptop must feel *so* good about themselves now. Watch out, Django.

— What is this django-django you keep blathering?

— Subbu! You don't remember when I caught Mansoor watching that porn film? Django Shanti? I bet he was fantasising about you.

— Stop making fun of the subaltern, ya.

I'd never heard the word 'subaltern' before I met Ajay. In a few months, I realised there were many, many ways in which it could be used. The first time I ever said something about servants, the whole group fell into shocked silence. Subbu told me carefully that nobody used the word 'servants' anymore. They were 'domestic help'. Varun, a fellow Malayali, whose favourite hobby was making jokes about Malayalis, said, making a face like an aunty, 'Or as they say in Kottayam, "sahayi".' And the group roared with laughter.

Ajay and Teresa's friends never stopped talking. They could not stop talking. They all spoke four, five languages, Malayalam, French, German, Spanish. At one point, three of them hired an Urdu tutor together so they could read poetry. But they were astonished when they found that I could speak Marathi. 'But I've lived in Bombay ten years. Don't any of you speak Marathi?' I asked mildly. After a three-second silence, someone made a joke about Raj Thackeray. Subbu reminded the others of the night Teresa had gone around stealing the Marathi signboards of pubs. That was the end of my brief superiority. Most of the time, I was on my phone, held discreetly under the table, googling things they were talking about so I didn't look like a blank-faced idiot.

Subbu had this thing. She would catch me on Gtalk and complain that she never got to hang out with me alone. She'd fix a date and place to meet after an elaborate negotiation and sign off saying how excited she was. Then, on the assigned day, she would send me a message saying she was terribly unwell or had a work crisis. And the next time she saw me online, she'd complain about how I was too busy to see her.

Early on, soon after she was back in the country, we did meet once. She took me to a very cool Pali Hill café, where there seemed to be famous people at every table. Through lunch she texted or chatted with friends at neighbouring tables. I watched her as if she was a very strange movie with subtitles, only occasionally able to focus on what she was saying to me. After a while, I realised that, more than anything else, she reminded me of people back home in Ranni.

— It must be strange for you. I told Ajay that we should talk less about school when you're around.

— Maybe you can persuade Ajay to write his book, finally. You know, long-form narrative journalism is the future. How long is he going to do this shit work for a bunch of Marwaris?

— My parents would have loved you. You are the kind of girl they must have dreamt of having before I was born. A bank job with gratuity. Do you have gratuity? Or maybe I mean PPF.

After Subbu's arrival, I spent less and less time with the group and no one really asked why. It wasn't cool for married couples in Ajay's circle to spend all their time together anyway. It was assumed that I had other things to do. I didn't, really. I'd become bored with my job. I mentioned to Ajay one day, some months after we got married, that people were getting laid off. Ajay told me to quit, we didn't need the money. It was true. We didn't need the money. I didn't tell Ajay and Teresa's friends I had quit my job. I noticed that Ajay had glossed over it too. His Valley School friends and Pallikudam friends and Oxford friends would never understand why I didn't have something going on, some project.

I wished I was the heroine in a makeover movie where I'd find a stylist and seduce my husband back. Only, in my case, my clothes were fine. For the first time, I was dressing as I wanted, buying the clothes I wanted. And I was not sure I wanted to seduce my husband into anything. I looked out of our windows at the sea and was terrified I'd wake up one morning and lose all this comfort, where no one asked me any questions. Even Mansoor-the-liar could be put off politely here.

I'm sure lots of people thought Ajay was marrying me to get a mother for Vinu, but I knew Ajay was the one who needed me. He had found a girl who looked on the outside like one of his people but would understand what he really wanted. So I stayed up late when he was out, ensured he ate on time, kept in touch with his parents and rationed his cigarettes a little bit. When he bought a Harley and kept it secret from his friends, I took my cue. When he told other people about it, I smiled and enjoyed their teasing. When he sold the Harley after never managing to put it on main stand without Mansoor's help, I kept that secret as well. In return, he never expected me to be anyone else.

Teresa had grown up in Brussels. This is the first thing I found out when I googled her years ago, before she died. School in Brussels, a few years in the US and art school in Berlin before moving to Bombay. I saw a picture of her on her German school's website. Already, you could see how tall she was going to be, as tall as her Belgian classmates, someday to be a stunning Amazon Malayali in Bombay. Teresa had been brought up by her diplomat aunt after her parents died in a car crash somewhere in America.

She had written for a few newspapers abroad, pieces about art and theatre. By the time she married Ajay, Teresa had become a strange combination: someone who wrote the news and someone who was the news. You know the girls in short dresses you saw every day in the *Times of India*, toasting the camera and laughing. Teresa was the girl some of them wanted to be. She was charismatic, brilliant and funny. She was everywhere and everyone knew her. All this I already knew by googling her over the years—long before I married Ajay or even met him.

I was the careful, polite second wife who asked Mansoor to dust the dead first wife's pictures while avoiding his greedy eyes. Some of my former colleagues who visited exclaimed about how so many of Teresa's photos were still all over the apartment and her name was still on the front door, but they hushed quickly when they saw my expression. That was in the first few months. Soon after, they faded out of my life along with my bank job, formal salwars and bank-job formal pants.

All this was before I opened Teresa's laptop. I had seen it several times, an old white Mac. On it, Teresa had painted a shimmering brown girl, naked except for her gold nose stud. The Mac had been put away along with some of her sketchbooks on a shelf in her study, a room she'd converted out of the balcony. The study was full of plants with enormous leaves that Mansoor looked after as if they were children. One day, I waited for Mansoor to be out of the flat to fish the Mac off the shelf. I had no problem figuring the silly password Teresa had given it. At the bank, I'd constantly be amazed at how clever people thought they were being with their security. They might as well have left the key to their house under a flower pot.

I logged in, and a week later, I dreamt of Teresa for the first time.

There was a girl in boarding school who, during the holidays, used to tell me everything about her life, every last detail. She used to call me every evening at my parents' friends' house to whine and complain and joke and bitch about everyone at school. She would stop calling the day before school reopened. In school, she never talked to me. I never asked. I just had to wait until the next holidays. When I read Teresa's secret blog, I heard the words in that girl's heated little voice.

Teresa's secret blog was not as old as the art blog, which everyone knew about and which by now was like a dargah for Teresa. This secret blog was on a carefully neutral template and had a silly name—Girl with a One Crack Mind. It didn't link to anything or anyone the public Teresa could be identified with. But she updated the secret blog avidly. Waiting for me to arrive years later.

Along the sun-drenched roadside, from the great
hollow half-tree trunk, which for generations
has been a trough, renewing in itself
an inch or two of rain, I satisfy
my thirst: taking the water's pristine coolness
into my whole body through my wrists.
Drinking would be too powerful, too clear;

but this unhurried gesture of restraint
fills my whole consciousness with shining water.
Thus, if you came, I could be satisfied
to let my hand rest lightly, for a moment,
lightly, upon your shoulder or your breast.

This was the poem Ajay had sent Teresa that had excited her enough to sleep with him. It took me a while to understand the poem, but there were lots of online poetry tutorials that explained it clearly. Teresa, of course, wouldn't have needed any explanations. She'd been excited that Ajay knew the Rilke poem, knew it in the original German.

The day Teresa slept with Ajay for the first time, she broke off her relationship with another man. In the early morning, she slept with Ajay. In the late evening, she slept with the other man and said goodbye to him. 'What a pity, since I had finally trained him,' she wrote. This, I imagined, she could have said on her public blog as well and her fans would have found it 'just like Teresa'.

In her columns for the papers and her public website, Teresa frequently implied that she was invincible, seemingly unbothered by anything. On the secret, and frequently tedious, blog, she was irritated by everybody. She used some fairly obvious nicknames for all her friends. Several descriptions of Subaltern Sub who was driving her crazy with her stupidity. Over the years, Teresa had bitched about almost all the people who claimed to be her bestest friends, her oldest friends. I had amused myself earlier by watching the memorial video Subbu had made after Teresa's death. After finding Teresa's blog, I watched it again and with greater amusement. I realised that even her every-night-at-Zenzi friends, and many others, had hedged on the video by saying they didn't know her well. As if they had just discovered that. But Teresa had known them all well.

I imagined Teresa sitting with the laptop at her dining table, typing up her blog posts, smiling sunnily across at Ajay working on his column or on the phone with his staff. He would not know she was describing his energetic but, to her, predictable tendencies in bed for her secret audience. That she took pleasure in sitting near him while typing about her newest lover.

One post fascinated me. I went to it over and over again. It was just a bunch of words. A list.

Orphans
Hunger hunger
Hate hate
Age
The one I beat
Twitchy Twitchy

This list called to me for some reason. As much as her detailed descriptions of cheating on Ajay. She wrote about men she wanted to sleep with, men she wanted to cut, men she wanted to bleed for. For a woman everyone said was impulsive, someone always described as being on her own trip, she had planned a lot.

I copied her hard drive on to mine and started digging around at leisure. Frequent links, online handles, favourite blogs, what she bought on eBay. Over the next few weeks, I would get to know all of them. But I loved the schoolgirl confidences of One Crack Mind girl the best. Did that woman at the parlour really make Teresa orgasm with a touch when she was getting a bikini wax? Did Teresa subtly create a rift between a married couple she met in Ranni because she was bored one holiday? I wasn't always sure what was true and what was Teresa's imagination.

She was sometimes attracted to some of the silent men who worked in and around the neighbourhood—the cleaners, the drivers, the couriers. 'What a tiresome cliché,' she wrote. 'But they are quiet. How grateful I am that they are quiet. How grateful that they have the hots for me without understanding a single word I say.'

One evening, when I clicked through Teresa's list of favourite links, I found a pondy photocomic that made my eyes water from all its variations of sexual positions. In bed that night, I irritated Ajay with my fits of giggles.

After Vinu was born, she wrote a few times in her public blog about being a mother. She raised what even I could see were the fashionable intellectual debates about motherhood. But it was on the secret blog that she wrote about the baby leaving her exhausted and angry. I couldn't stop smiling when I saw those posts, knowing Teresa would never publicly admit to being defeated by anything as small and banal as a baby.

She wrote about swimming often and how much she loved it. Of the sun beating down on her red eyelids when she was floating on her back. I wondered often how an expert swimmer had drowned in the pool one afternoon, but who was I, Nancy Drew?

One evening, Ajay invited the gang home for dinner. Mansoor was in top form, telling Bihari jokes, making kababs and racing out, buying tender coconuts and filling them with vodka and sugar. Everyone was, very quickly, drunk.

Subbu had brought Ajay a pile of books from Mexico. She was exuberant in a way I now imagined she probably could never have been while Teresa was around. While vivaciously exclaiming over one of the books, she said, 'It's a very lush novel, obsessed with aesthetics and allegories. A grand passion. Like yours and Teresa's. She'd have loved…', and began to weep quietly. Everyone ran across the living room to comfort her but not before I saw her eyes glancing fish-like to see how I was taking it.

I went into the bedroom and came back with one of my white handkerchiefs and gave it to her. I brought her water and sat beside her, saying nothing, knowing that my simple proximity was giving her an allergy attack. Her fake grief was turning into nervous agitation. And just when I thought she was close to cracking, I got up. I went to the balcony and looked out at the sea. Ajay came quietly to see if I was okay. I was laughing on the inside, but he didn't know that. I was sure Teresa would have laughed at Subaltern Sub's elaborate pretensions too.

The next time Ajay invited everyone over, Subbu insisted she didn't want to hang out in anyone's house.

She wanted to go out. Back we were at Zenzi. Subbu was carefully polite with me, but when no one was looking, I saw her mouth droop in irritation, dissatisfaction. I went to the loo, looked in the mirror while washing my hands and I saw Teresa standing behind me in a short yellow dress, her curls glossy and her lips smirking red.

For a while, I tried to stop digging into Teresa's online life, worrying I was going crazy. But it was just for a few days. The moment Mansoor would leave the flat after lunch, I'd tuck into bed with Teresa, reading everything she had to say. Years of Facebook updates. Drafts for her articles. To-do lists. Her accounts. Birthday reminders. The graphic novel she kept starting and stopping. Her heroine Tara's breasts changed in size in each draft but she remained unbeatable in her ability to seduce men and women.

When I stumbled on her secret Flickr account, even I, Teresa's last and bestest friend, was amazed. She'd spent a lot of time photographing herself from the neck down. There were lots of pictures she'd taken in the house and in other places I didn't recognise. They were strange angles, so I imagined they were taken on her digital camera or phone. I imagined her propping her camera up or holding the phone out with her long, lean arms. She had photographed everything. Birthmarks and veins. Dark damp bits. Pale parts unexposed to the sun. The one link on her blog about these photos that I found after some searching was a single-line entry: 'So that I remember that I was all this.' I saw the sweat she had carefully photographed on her own clavicle and the crease of her thighs, and felt dizzy. The tips of my fingers tingled and my bare legs felt liquid. I switched off the AC, opened the windows and curtains. I lay naked in bed letting the sunlight touch me.

Vinu's arrival in the house changed almost everything. Walking around with Vinu changed the neighbourhood for me. Strangers smiled at us. Some friends, a lot of Ajay's friends, were more ambivalent when they visited. It was not a coincidence that Vinu's first venture when graduating from genteel Malayalam into pert English was, 'I don't like children.'

Ajay walked carefully around him to begin with. But as he discovered his son—as much in love with words as he was, as precocious as he and Teresa had been—Ajay began to stay at home more. The house was crowded with new visitors, overnight guests. In December that year, we had guests from abroad every week. They were Teresa's friends who all wanted to meet Vinu. Ajay spoke only in Malayalam to Vinu, teasing me that I was going to give Vinu a wretched, lisping Non-Resident Malayali accent. It was true that Ajay's alternative school upbringing had given him more Malayalam than my old-fashioned boarding schools. One of Ajay's Valley School friends said something about sending Vinu there, and I told him to shut up. Vinu was going to grow up at home with us. My status as full-time mother was now public.

I rarely had time for Teresa now, but I waited desperately to be alone with her laptop. After a while without her friendship, it became difficult for me to be my efficient self with Ajay in bed. That is when I began to dream of her every night.

When I was a child, I used to cry imagining my parents dead. When I was fifteen and they hung themselves, I didn't cry. As an adult, my tears always take me by surprise. Odd things make me cry. Young families eating in restaurants: I see the tired shoving of food into their mouths and I feel like weeping. Of course, after marrying Ajay, I've rarely been in a restaurant where anyone looked tired.

One day, I saw Ajay sitting on our balcony bent double in the dark, and I suddenly understood what he would be like as an old man. Shrunken and skinny. I'm sure young people will think of him as that cynical, funny journalist uncle who had once been so successful. But they'd never know how he danced. They would never be shocked by his dense chest hair, so unexpected on someone so smooth-skinned, which showed on the rare occasion when his second button was open. They would never know his small body had never affected his success with women everywhere he went. All that the young people in Ajay's future would know is a small, birdlike old person's body.

For the first time in our life together, I reached over and hugged him. Squeezed him hard. Imagined hugging the old man he would become. I could feel tears, but the question that popped out of my mouth surprised me more than the tears.

'Do you miss her?'

Ajay stayed silent.

I said, 'I'm sure you felt like Rilke with Teresa.' I could almost hear him stop breathing in shock, so I don't know why I went on. 'I would have wanted to rest my hand lightly on her shoulder too.'

Last night I dreamt of Teresa again.

The Gentle Reader

BANGALORE

Four years ago, Sabbah had written eleven short stories about different generations of a family in Madurai. At the time that she submitted it to publishers, Sabbah had loved most of the stories. When ten of the stories were selected and arranged into a book called *How to Eat in Madurai, Mami*, she had still loved the stories. When the book finally reached the public, two years later, the delay had taken the gloss off a bit.

During the wait, it had become difficult for her not to snarl at acquaintances in Bangalore who earnestly asked her how much her advance had been and whether in her 'professional opinion' *The White Tiger* deserved the Booker. As a writer who hadn't been published yet, she told herself, she was not required to have an opinion or to be gracious. She was not required to be anything.

During the wait, it seemed to her that the publishing house was run by strange, contrary women who sent her emails deliberately strewn with grammatical errors. The woman who called her most often had a conversational tic of saying 'fair enough' when nothing was being debated, driving Sabbah into a disproportionate rage. Another woman mailed her asking for her bio every three months (or so it seemed). Yet another wrote to her objecting to the titles of her stories ('Your titles have literary resonance but don't mean anything') and to her photo ('Your photo does not have any literary resonance').

Then, when she had almost given up, a writer friend recommended that she 'sign up with one of these new agents'. Sabbah, who'd thought that all literary agents were Jewish and lived in New York, was pleased at the prospect of meeting such an entity. (She had loved *Joys of Yiddish* and often gifted copies to people who she thought would appreciate the economy of wickedness in Yiddish.) Three email conversations and a trip to Delhi later, she had signed with an agent.

She was secretly disappointed that, far from being colourful and rude, her agent was a pleasant, well-spoken middle-aged woman called Shakuntala. The agent was of indeterminate North Indian origin and habitually wore smart trousers. She was vegetarian, and when Sabbah asked her whether she found it difficult to be so in Delhi, she responded, 'Food is not a priority for me. I find eating boring.' Sabbah, who lived in a city where people customarily greeted each other by asking whether they'd eaten, was quelled.

Whether it was the briskness of her agent or cosmic timing, she didn't know, but a month later, her publisher suddenly woke up. Nothing would do but for the book to be out that month. She even got a miffed email reprimanding her for delaying the process by not organising her photo for the dust jacket.

Suddenly, the book (stories, jacket, price, photo, cover design, copyright, her name) was out in shops (well, some). Her friends had made a game of marching into Bangalore bookshops and loudly demanding the book. Unfortunately, Sabbah herself was not so proud of the book anymore. Her historical research was excellent, but her prose, she thought now, was Dolly Partonesque—big-haired and over the top. Sabbah read the stories for the first time in two years. She was more than a little horrified at how arch some of them seemed. It would have been better, she thought now, to be a *bad* writer than to be *arch*. She was a whisker away from *twee*. Every cliché that had ever been claimed about Indian writers seemed to be there. Mango-monsoon-pudding, she spat at herself.

But the publishing house offered her a second book 'if she had any ideas, preferably historical'.

'Ideas? Do you have any?' Shakuntala wanted to know on the phone. There was more than a hint of impatience in her voice.

Sabbah panicked. If she said she had no ideas, would the offer of the second book vanish? Forever?

'Well, I had this one idea. There is a character from the second story, she is a very minor character, but I think…interesting. Jamuna, the Gujarati bride?'

'Hmm.'

'Yes, the Gujarati bride is brought to Madurai in the 1800s. I had hinted that she is from a shipping family. I thought I could develop a novel around her...about how her family were originally slave traders and how they change from that...'

'Hmmm,' said Shakuntala. 'Send me an email. It sounds workable. Don't be like Vikram Chandra and take eight years, though.' Shakuntala was not joking. Sabbah resented how little joking there seemed to be in publishing.

Fuelled by panic and the chance to redeem herself, Sabbah dashed off a proposal. A few months later, she was in business again. Which is to say that she had a year, a tiny potli of money and leave from her teaching job to write her first novel. When things got, she found herself in terror. The research itself was fairly tough. And then there was the writing. Had she been insane to agree to do it in a year? When she couldn't even get short stories straight, what kind of effort would it take to finish a novel? What kind of publisher made it so easy for any moron to get published? The bad kind. Terrible people who didn't care about books.

Gritting her teeth, she wrote to libraries around the country requesting permission to work in their archives. For her first stint of research, Sabbah went to Mumbai.

MUMBAI

There was a certain glamour in being in Mumbai as a writer and not a reader. On a day filled with breeze, sunshine and Gothic architecture, could you be unhappy?

Every day, she took the fast train to town from her friend's flat in Andheri and found a new place to eat breakfast. Then she strolled to the Asiatic Society library, ridiculously replete with the luxury of being a writer. How wonderful, how illicit to sit somewhere and scratch one's itches.

In this new upbeat mood, Jamuna, the central character of her book, was unfortunately, already annoying. In the evenings, when Sabbah tried her hand at some writing, she found her heroine passive-aggressive and dull. Part of this was circumstantial. Sabbah did not believe in historically inaccurate emancipation for characters in historical novels. She could not make Jamuna hate her family's slave-trading business to fit a more modern, more liberal narrative. In the one para Jamuna got in the short story, she fell in love with a Tamilian clerk and ventured across the subcontinent to live in a temple town where no one spoke her language. And that had pretty much used up her supply of courage. So why write about Jamuna? And if she didn't care about Jamuna's feelings, who would?

In her second week at the library, she was choked. Somewhere in this building, she had been told, is an actual manuscript of *The Divine Comedy*. Dante Alighieri had not sat around in the 1300s writing coy shit. Somewhere near here, Arun Kolatkar had written *Jejuri* and the *Kala Ghoda* poems. Somewhere near here, Kolatkar had died. Where in her writing was the blood, the grime, the puking on the streets and the deep stuff?

She had agreed too fast to the publisher's offer and now her name would be mud.

Sabbah slid off to an Irani restaurant to eat berry pulao. She grinned weakly when the owner reprimanded her for eating too slowly. 'You are slower than a snail, young lady,' complained the octogenarian bending over her table. 'Daddy!' yelled his middle-aged son from behind the large cat on his cash counter. Mommy, thought Sabbah.

She went back to the Asiatic Library and would perhaps have got some work done if she had not accidentally stumbled on a collection of well-preserved posters advertising Victorian freak shows. Always a sucker for lowbrow Victoriana, she fell straight in.

Most of her subsequent weeks in Mumbai were wasted in getting better acquainted with the febrile enterprise of P.T. Barnum, the American showman who prided himself on freak shows for the entire Victorian family. She spent hours staring at the posters, enjoying their typography and their unselfconscious invitation to people to come and stare.

And that is how Sabbah caused Jamuna's early demise.

BANGALORE

> 'But who is there that abstains from reading
> that which is printed in abuse of himself?'
>
> – *Phineas Finn*, Anthony Trollope

in her. How had she got herself into this? And why were people saying nice things about her stories? Whatever happened to taste?

The designer, who was trying to become a social media consultant, threw in a Twitter account. Shakuntala thought she could use Twitter to post notes, one-liners and anecdotes as she researched the book. 'It could be good build-up for the novel,' she reasoned. 'All the movie stars are doing it. You know, fun stuff from the sets, their diets, costumes, dance sequences.'

Sabbah should have pointed out that anything she found interesting would hopefully go into the book. Instead, she fell upon Twitter.

'At painful times, when composition is impossible and reading is not enough, grammars and dictionaries are excellent for distraction,' Elizabeth Barrett Browning had written to her novelist pal Mary Russell Mitford. But that was only because Liz and Mary didn't have Twitter, thought Sabbah.

To begin with, she posted little one-liners and photos from her research on *How To Eat in Madurai, Mami*. Three days later, someone replied to a tweet. Sabbah stared at it for a long while and then read it again. She was hooked. This person from Lucknow had actually read her book. After having resisted blogging for a whole decade, she was sucked in by a forty-eight-character message from a person in a gorilla mask.

Who was this person? Why did he or she like her book? What else did he or she read? Sabbah spent a

Back in Bangalore, she was aware that her year was slipping away and that no significant work had been done. Bored already with Jamuna's frequently bathing in-laws and the unrelieved cruelty of her slave-trading family, Sabbah fantasised about writing a Victorian murder mystery instead.

'I would be Sarah Waters but with fewer lesbians, Anne Perry with less stiff upper lip, A.S. Byatt but not so annoying,' she rhapsodised to her friend Menaka.

'But you've never even been to England.'

'What about H.R.F. Keating?' argued Sabbah.

There was, of course, no rejoinder to this. If H.R.F. Keating could write nine of his twenty-four Inspector Ghote stories, all set in a living and breathing Mumbai, before ever setting foot in India and without the benefit of the Internet, then anyone could write anything.

At this point, she found to her excruciating embarrassment that *How to Eat in Madurai, Mami* began doing reasonably well. She saw a few copies with a pavement hawker. A well-known journalist mentioned it in passing on an odds-and-ends culture show on TV. A publisher (not her own) called her one of the few Indian writers worth reading.

A designer pal then had the happy idea of promoting *How to Eat in Madurai, Mami* and the forthcoming novel by creating a website with the genealogy of the Madurai family. 'The soaring saga of one Madurai family who acquires a Gujarati bride in the 18th century,' Sabbah read on her website. She knew that no soaring saga was few hours wandering the net, always returning to the comment. '@MaduraiMami Enjoyed your short stories. Thanks'

The next morning, she jumped up and logged into Twitter. There were no new interactions. By evening, there were a couple of retweets. She couldn't stop grinning. Over the next week, many more appeared.

Not all the tweets were milk and honey. There was a man from Madurai who stormed at her for the one paragraph of sex in one of the ten stories. Sabbah tried to laugh it off, but was uncomfortably aware again that someone, someone who was not her friend, had read her book and judged her life and character by it.

Over the next few weeks, the half-hearted conversations turned into an unexpectedly angry one. Someone from Ahmedabad announced that she had a history of anti-Gujarati sentiment. As proof he offered this: 'See her name on top of this petition. bit.ly/ch/1652d'

Followed by: 'See the kind off pseudo-sickular anti-national things Indian English writers do. All for publicity'

Sabbah saw that @S_Vohra had indeed found an old petition she had signed online right after the Gujarat riots.

Then, a week later, @S_Vohra tweeted a link to his long, befuddling analysis of the jacket design of *How to Eat in Madurai, Mami*. If you stood upside down and squinted at the cover, it looked like Om with devil's horns. The minority was always trying to provoke, felt S_Vohra.

She was tempted to defend herself, but the online conversation caught fire and didn't need her intervention at all. The liberals had found her on Twitter. Only occasionally would her haters or defenders remember that the stories had anything to do with their bitter rants.

Three days later, the thread ran out. But a new one began criticising her writing abilities and her understanding of the world. She went from anxious to depressed.

SirPachkao tweeted: 'I googled you and saw some of your old photos. So, dear, what's the truth? Publishers photoshop your ugly face?' He continued, 'Or did you get some big-ass plastic surgery. Because that picture on the bookjacket (which I still want a refund for btw) ain't you.'

She went determinedly to bed. Half an hour later, she got out of bed and went looking for a copy of her book and turned to her photograph. It was certainly flattering. A little too flattering? She squinted at it. Was that really her?

It wasn't her. Was it?

Her nondescript face varied widely in photographs but this jaw was someone else's. But how could that be? It did look different in this light. She went into the bathroom, switched on two sets of lights and examined her jaw again. Outrage bloomed. Had they really photoshopped her for the book jacket? No, they couldn't have.

Sabbah flew out of the bathroom in horror and jumped into bed and moaned aloud. She jumped out of bed and hopped around. And moaned louder. She would have yelled if she didn't think her poor neighbours would wake up and call her.

She went to sleep. Woke at 1 a.m. and looked at her laptop sleeping quietly in the corner of the bed. She burrowed her way through the bed cover and opened it. Go to sleep, she told herself. But she had to see if there were any new tweets.

There were.

SirPachkao: 'Your writing is terrible, dear, and no one would buy your book. I still want my money back.' And later: 'I don't mind too much though because the bookshops have stopped stocking your sucky book.'

V_Krishna: 'Your writing sheer verbal diarhia as your head is empty.'

SirPachkao making friends and influencing people: '@MaduraiMami @V_krishna don't be fooled. This book is part of a deliberate campaign to denigrate Hinduism.'

And from there it went rather downhill. SirPachkao had an elaborate explanation for why he thought all her Hindu characters were slave traders and evil. It was because she was funded by foreign NGOs and the ISI to hurt the sentiments of Hindus.

At some point, the fight shifted to her Facebook author page.

V_Krishna: 'This iz kalyug. However it's not going to last long. The end of creation iz not very far. With militant Islam surging chaos is take over our whole world. Ending to the world iz predicted in scriptures. End will be preceded by appearance of the Bhagwan in his final avatar…Kalki Avatar. What must happen will happen. As they say, nobody can stop an idea the time for which has come!'

SirPachkao, of course, had jumped in there too: 'But we must stop Sabbah's kind of writing. Anti-Brahminism prospers in anti-Hindu circles. It is welcome among Marxists, missionaries, Muslims, terrorists and Christian-backed Dalit movements of different shades and hues. When these people attack Brahmins, their target is actually Hinduism.'

Arjun Parameswaran: 'You guys are unbelievable idiots. Can't believe the crap you are writing. Don't like the book, don't buy it. And Kalki is with Anurag.'

Rohit Pandey: 'Dalits will be given every opportunity to rise but a Brahmin will be given every opportunity to fall. Met many Dalits in the workplace. Most of them are revengeful. Worst charecteristcs any human can have is in them.'

As a writer, Sabbah thought, she was committed to the notion that evil exists in the world. But even she was not ready for the evil she was discovering on the net.

Next week, Menaka quoted Kurt Vonnegut at her: 'Any reviewer who expresses rage and loathing for a novel is like a person who has put on full armour and attacked a hot fudge sundae.'

'But that's not the problem here. They are calling *me* a hot fudge sundae.'

'I thought they were calling you a slut.'

'That was last week. This week is the languid, sophisticated heckler week. They're calling me stupid.'

Menaka laughed and changed the subject. Sabbah, who worried that she was a bore, was happy to go along.

But when she got home she saw that SirPachkao, the leader of the headless horsemen, had made fresh sorties.

She thought it was wrong to block trolls just because she did not agree with them, but after two weeks of these comments and an intern from a Chennai tabloid calling her about the 'brewing controversy around her book', any sense of moderation left her. She was ready to block and tackle all around. She deliberately avoided logging in for three days. Soon, she told herself, she would be away in the hills at a literary festival. Some respite.

But the night before she was due to leave for McLeod Ganj, she caved and logged in. It was unfortunate that her aunt in Chennai finally reached her right then, dying to talk about the article in the tabloid. Sabbah was freshly irritated and the ganas were waiting with buckets of shit.

SirPachkao: 'Come out, come out. Didn't you feminists burn your bras to meet us at the same level? Why are you hiding now?'

V_Krishna: 'Maybe she iz feeling shy like girlz from my village.'

SirPachkao: 'If you had got married and had a few children then you wouldn't have all these problems.'

SirPachkao: 'I see from yr FB account that yr younger cousins are also unmarried. Planning to make them Madrasi lesbos like you?'

Later on, Sabbah would wonder why that particular permutation of the classroom taunt had been the one to make her break her self-imposed silence. Or perhaps it was the horrific realisation SirPachkao might be her

Facebook 'friend' using an alias. Before she could think, she typed:

'@SirPachkao It's that kind of thinking that ensures dirty cowbelt North Indians like you don't have any women to marry.'

'@SirPachkao After killing them you have to go everywhere else in India and buy women to cook and clean and bear your ugly children.'

Oh god, what a fucking mistake.

But it was too late. It took her a minute to regret her rage and delete her two tweets. By then she had been retweeted thrice and Pachkao had responded. A smug little comment: '@MaduraiMami Well, well, there goes the pseudo-sickular.... Who is the liberal now?'

Dammit, dammit! The moral high ground had been well and truly lost. At least no one could see her comment now. Without thinking too much she blocked @SirPachkao. It stared at her freedom-of-speech-loving face.

New tweets.

Sockpuppet: 'Hey why're u so down on the guy? He's been making interesting points. You're being really f-ed up about it, blocking him. Pardon my French.'

Sabbah looked narrowly at this comment. How did he know I blocked SirPachkao? Who said, 'Pardon my French'? Sure, this country's Anglophone landscape was filled with archaisms, but 'Pardon my French'! Who said that? She suspected This Guy was also That Guy. This seemed like a fake identity that SirPachkao had made to support himself. Or maybe there really were people who supported Pachkao. Of course there were people who supported Pachkao. The world was full of crazies.

Someone called Kakakakiran was helpfully RTing screenshots of her original tweets over and over again.

Sockpuppet: 'Bro, I can't believe she said that. @MaduraiMami, what the f is your problem?'

Kakakakiran: 'All these Arundhati Roy wannabes are all bitches.'

Vir_Bir_Batra: 'Fuck you, deleting the tweet after saying what you want. At least we North Indians are brave. We protect you from pakistani, you madrasis.'

S_Vohra: 'All this time I was telling you she is anti-Gujarat and you never listened. Serves you right.'

Arjunnotthewarrior: '@MaduraiMami what did you say to make all the trolls wake up?'

S Vohra: '@Arjunnotthewarrior She called someone a dirty, unwashed cowbelt North Indian.'

Arjunnotthewarrior: 'No way, @MaduraiMami is this true?'

S Vohra: 'All true and now hiding behind the block, yeah lady?'

Arjunnotthewarrior: '@MaduraiMami This is really shocking.'

Vinu298: '@Arjunnotthewarrior What's so shocking? North indians are useless. All the forex earnings in this country because of south india. BPOs, KPOs and IT.'

Sakshilove: 'Completely uncalled for @MaduraiMami. Bad enough that our communal politicians are saying it but educated people like you? Please apologise.'

Mami thought she should, but she was damned if she was going to.

Minissha_Arora: 'Sabbah, I can't believe you are such a bigot. Your true colours are showing now.'

Minissha_Arora: 'Can't believe you've been hiding your ill-informed prejudices all this while. I can't believe you ever visited my home.'

Who the hell was Minissha Arora? The name vaguely rang a bell.

Sakshilove: 'She was in your house? I think we should boycott her and her book. I always knew it was a bad book.'

Sabbah closed the window, switched off the computer and tried to sleep. She had two hours before her cab would arrive for the airport.

On the road, she was ill with anxiety and lack of sleep. She had packed three books for the trip but couldn't concentrate on any. After checking in, as if she couldn't help herself, she downloaded Twitter on her phone. There were eighteen new tweets mentioning her. She couldn't bear to read them. She couldn't bear to sit in the plane and not know what was being said. By the time the call to the gate came, she'd deleted the app from her phone. She had stopped after reading the first tweet. Something about five ways to lose that stubborn belly fat.

MCLEOD GANJ

How much would it cost to rent an elephant for the day?
Here?

No, back in Delhi. It would be the most ironic experience to Instagram.

Bryan's friend can arrange it. Just ask.

The textile dealer guy? Really?

I think the operative word is dealer.

Aah, I see.

Sabbah added goras to the list of people she hated. She also added people whose English was gora-like. All her life she'd adored complex sentences in English. Now she'd settle for grunts without irony or allusion, anything but this feathery chatter.

No one-book-old writer should go to literary festivals, Sabbah thought. There were next to no readers here. She was not expecting to see *fans*. But there were no readers. She'd been excited when she first realised she was going to a literary festival — for the first time in her life she'd be surrounded by her own kind. But the Twitter drama was making her so anxious she couldn't enjoy anything. And two days in, she could see that she may not have liked the event anyway.

By lunchtime on the third day Sabbah understood. She'd confused writers with book lovers. Where the book lover wanted you to please, please read this new book, this old favourite, ('You'll love it, it would be a favour to me'), writers were shit scared and Scrooge-like. She told herself not to be a naïf. Nothing more annoying than an overage ingénue.

The lit fest was not in McLeod Ganj but a couple of kilometres uphill in a smaller village. The events were all scheduled in and around a hotel set well back on a wide, green cliff. Stalls selling books and souvenirs were set up around the lawns, without obscuring the view in any manner. People drifted in and out of the hotel coffee shop and the panel discussions. It should have been an omen to her that not one of the hundreds of people in expensive winter clothing were at the edge of the cliff gawking at the Dhauladars. In the taxi, driving down, she'd been distracted by the autumn colours of everyone's clothes as they floated like butterflies with wineglasses.

Today, on the third day, she got herself some coffee and stood with a vacant half-smile, ready to convert to a full one for any comers. Her stomach still threatened to heave every time she thought about what fresh hell was brewing on her Twitter timeline. Sabbah had switched off her phone after she saw missed calls from *The Times of India*. She imagined her parents' home in Bangalore being attacked by some Hindutva gang. But for now she'd pretend that she was just another writer on a junket.

Shakuntala came over in a russet silk outfit and introduced her to a middle-aged woman, a writer from Chennai, who was now teaching in the American Midwest. The woman was polite though not warm. Since she had three fairly successful books out in the world, Sabbah listened to everything she said attentively.

The writer said, 'I must admit I'm quite excited about my new book. It will be the first time a hijra is the central character of a novel.'

Oh, said Sabbah, riding up gaily in her clown car, 'Oh, there've been two books like that already. That man from Kerala and that new British novel…' She had blurted out everything short of the ISBN numbers of the two books before she noticed that the writer was not too pleased to not be the 'first' she'd imagined. She left with a hint of flounce to her phiran.

Sabbah was mortified. Standing there, letting conversations wash over her head, she felt like crying.

'Why can't Indians write about anything other than themselves? Why can't they write about being a Chinese empress or something?'

'It's easy enough for Willie. He probably hops into his car and is driven to the Archives. They'll open everything, including the loo door, for him. While we have to fight through red tape and hope for a sniff at some good material.'

'David Lodge really was right. It's exactly like in *Small World*. The academic circuit and the literary circuit. It's just the same. The rich writers get more residencies, more festival invitations, offers to teach, offers to speak.'

'If he were dead, he'd make such a good book. Sherlock Holmes pastiche writer, former CIA guerrilla, now living in exile. Is it true that he's here? It'd be fantastic to meet him.'

'He's a very good person, an excellent writer, but he'll never finish that novel. It's been six years since he got the advance. Now he doesn't even answer the phone if he sees it's a Delhi number.'

'Of course the meltdown is going to happen any minute now. These advances are completely unrealistic.'

'What advances? Nobody gets advances any more. The meltdown has happened. You just missed it living in Amsterdam.'

'What the fuck is an impresario anyway?'

One writer holding a pre-lunch glass of wine as big as his head informed Sabbah, 'I am unfashionably erudite.' Sabbah guffawed. When she looked at the writer's broad, sullen face, she realised that he'd meant it. She stuttered wildly and ran away looking for human beings. But they were all, in her Hindi teacher's words, namoonas. Each and every one.

Then, around lunchtime, she had a long, calming conversation with a tall woman holding the hand of a sulking five-year-old girl. They discussed the weather, shopping in McLeod Ganj, the view, treks, the Dalai Lama, until Sabbah caught the woman looking across the lawn angrily at a tall, neat man a few metres away.

'That's my husband. He's a writer too.' His was a book that Sabbah had liked. But she sensed that to praise the book would be to end this pleasant conversation. She bent down to talk to the now quiet child. When she looked up again, the woman's anger had faded into resignation.

Later, alone again with her thoughts about the hundreds of incoherent messages probably flaming her Twitter timeline right now, she walked determinedly out of the hall and hailed the only taxi in sight.

As she left, she saw the newest star of the non-fiction scene screaming into his phone. His eyes were bulging.

'Fuck off, fuck off, I'll never review a book for you again, you bitch.' She hurried past him, thankful that her youthful enthusiasm for drama in public seemed to have faded. Was that what she'd looked like as a teenager crying in STD booths and autos?

Five minutes later, she was hurtling at high speed down Tipa Road back to McLeod Ganj. Speeding on mountain curves was good in the movies and in life. All along she caught glimpses of grinning pedestrians saluting her foolhardy taxi driver. But why couldn't she feel better? She got up on her knees on the taxi seat and dangled her upper body out of the window. The driver, intent on his satanic race downhill, barely spared her a glance. Only iron determination stopped her from leaping out of the window entirely. She needed bodily mortification or elevation of some sort to wake her from this fugue.

But was it a fugue, really? Was it boredom and impatience with these unimpressive specimens of humanity? Or was it just the fear that soon she'd be shamed and exposed as a fraud?

Too insecure to pursue that thought any further, she was glad to find herself in McLeod Ganj, a town that had always made her happy when it had been base camp for treks. She got out of the taxi and began walking up Temple Street, the main road. No more than four people could walk side-by-side here. Sabbah knew she should keep her eyes open to see the underbelly of tourism, but it was difficult to think dark thoughts with the scene currently unfolding before her.

The fat jewellery-seller's Lhasa Apso had liberated itself. As she watched, people up and down the street dropped what they were doing and chased the puppy. Up the road, behind a man in a cowboy hat, two monks, one blind, one sighted, examined a length of meat and bargained with the butcher whose shop was, literally, a large cupboard set into a stone wall. Far away from writers, the world functioned steadily and happily.

About to burst into sentimental tears, Sabbah escaped into a café. Ogo's was orange on the outside. It had six orange tables and was as neat and as pretty as the inside of a music box. After all these years of visiting McLeod Ganj, Sabbah felt no need to look at the menu in any establishment. All of them had the same fare. She ordered ginger lemon tea, two plates of dimsums, a frittata and two kinds of cake.

Two hours later, she was in a deep food coma. She walked to her hotel at the slowest pace possible. Climbing the stairs was absolute agony with the world swinging blackly around her. A waiter she passed looked at her in scorn. Richard Gere had probably never come back to the hotel sloshing with food. She missed the Rs 500-a-night backpacker favourites with their draughty rooms and warm hosts.

Back in her room she fell asleep in a second. When she woke up, it was dark outside. She felt hollow, as if she would echo if someone shouted into her mouth. She felt ill, all thoughts paling from the overwhelming presence of her body.

The phone rang and it was Shakuntala wondering where she was. She took a taxi back to the festival and steeled herself to behave more maturely.

'Is it an Animal? Is it Human? Is it an Extraordinary Freak of Nature? Or is it a legitimate member of Nature's Work?'

– *The Illustrated London News*,
29 August 1846

The crowds were just thickening when she arrived. She settled down in a corner with an ample shawl, an equally ample Hilary Mantel and the determination to grin and bear it. In a few minutes, Shakuntala came over and introduced her young son Rishi, who had recently joined her agency. Rishi was hatta-katta, had spiky hair and the most extraordinarily white face. It was not the kind of fairness that everyone in India aspired to, this bloodless pallor. She smiled and made polite noises. Shakuntala's efficient genteelness intimidated her. But the literary agent asked for no explanations for Sabbah's disappearance and left to speak to someone else in a few minutes.

To her surprise, cold-faced young Rishi did not disappear immediately after introductions. He sat down beside her, began chatting and she willed herself to not feel grateful.

Before joining his mother's business, Rishi had worked in the country's biggest PR firm, the one that took care of Bollywood's brightest. His stories were, therefore, predictably full of adultery, cupidity and sleaze. But they were told with such disinterest that he seemed more ruthless than the most determined iconoclast, the most poisonous gossip-monger. She had to ask him to stop the endless supply, laughing to hide her dismay. Rishi looked at her as if he was not fooled, his serial-killer eyes at half-mast.

Rishi's friends came over as well. They were all young men and women with clear skin and perfect grooming. She thought with secret shame that in school this would have been the cool group that she could never have been a part of. With her mind running on these *Gossip Girl* lines, it didn't surprise her when she was offered hash brownies ('Retro cool,' a girl smirked).

'I love you, Alice B. Toklas,' Sabbah thought to herself and accepted one, feeling sad that, sober or stoned, she would not tell this group about the Toklas cookbook.

Two hours and four joints 'straight from Parvati Valley' later, she could only hope that no one, absolutely no one would speak directly to her. The end of sentences that she heard made no sense because she had forgotten their beginning. Her mind was in a thirty-second loop. Panic. What's happening to me? Oh yes, the weed. Ah, it'll end in a while. Panic. What's happening to me? Oh yes, the weed. Ah, it'll end in a while. Panic. What's happening to me? Oh yes, the weed. Ah, it'll end in a while.

Sometime later—it was difficult to estimate how much later—it seemed the party had truly begun. The level of noise and laughter and movement had increased in the lawns. She sat absolutely still looking only at people who came into her line of vision. And in her line of vision were people from exotic climes.

Moving wraith-like across the lawn were two thirteen-year-olds, easily the youngest writers there. Rumour had it that only one of the twins had written the *Wakawaka Asura* trilogy, but their astonishing success had them tied together at their coltish knees.

'They are huge in Europe. Also in Japan,' Rishi announced. 'The Japanese love identical twins and freaky shit.'

The world-renowned conjoined Siamese Twins, Chang and Eng, thought Sabbah, who had a sudden photographic recollection of the Piccadilly Hall poster that featured the twins in tailcoats shooting, rowing, fishing and riding horse carriages with the faux-aristocratic hauteur of all Victorian freaks.

Near the wine bar was a Hottentot Venus in a green shimmering sari, laughing sexily or frowning sexily at a dozen satellites. 'Like a wild beast, she was ordered to move backwards and forwards, and come out and go into her cage, more like a bear in a chain than a human being,' quoted Sabbah to whomsoever it may concern. Hot and taut, she giggled.

The young Pakistani writer Zulekha, too, had her own immodest orbit. She was pale-skinned with huge dark circles under her eyes. It was implied in gesture and soft voice that she had suffered as much as her memoirs said. She had fought and now she was free. From the zenana that oppressed her, of course. Sabbah looked at her silky pants, her Jimmy Choos and Cossack-style hat and thought: 'Circassian beauty, stolen from her home by white-slavers for an evil Turk who wanted an addition to his harem. She escaped with her life to tell her tale.' Zulekha, Zana Zanobia, Zoë Meleke, Zula, Zalumma Agra, Zoberdie Luti. Bring them all on, the dancing girls, giants, dwarfs, Siamese twins, hermaphrodites, fat ladies, living skeletons, wild men, noble savages.

The next one who appeared could have qualified as a giant but what he was, Sabbah knew instantly, was the Wild Man of Borneo. A fourth-generation Indian in Indonesia, he was somehow also the local go-to on all matters weighty in Indian culture. The press loved him because, during his twice-yearly appearances in India, he was guaranteed to say something inappropriate and delicious. She remembered how awed she was at nineteen when she'd first heard him speak, and tried to remember how it had felt.

Someone was talking to her. She looked owl-eyed at a young editor she had been introduced to on the first day of the festival.

'So man, everyone is buzzing about your Twitter war. Let's hope the newspapers don't see that latest tweet. It was all over the place before you deleted it. By the way, Minissha is saying she'll never talk to you again.' She smiled at Sabbah, who could barely form a sentence in her defence. Even stoned she knew she would never be able to defend herself for what she had said. And who was Minissha?

And just like that, she was gone.

Sabbah knew then that she was the freak show. She was the smallest person in the world. She wanted to shrink further and disappear.

Somehow she manoeuvred herself away from Rishi and friends, out of the hotel and to the taxi stand. For the second time that day, she was in a taxi rattling down Tipa Road, but nothing could make her feel better now. The taxi scraped the last few yards before hitting the centre of town. She could not bear to go back to the hotel, so she hopped off on Temple Street again. On an impulse, she went to one of the grocery stores that had posters for movie screenings. The shopkeeper, who was arranging cabbages in a basket, told her that yes, *I Know What You Did Last Summer* was due to start in a few minutes. He pocketed her Rs 40, moved aside two baskets of potatoes, unlatched a trapdoor in the floor and ushered her down a metal staircase into a basement.

It was exactly what a movie hall ought to be but in miniature. There was the slight slope down to the screen and rows of cushioned seats. It could have seated forty people but there were only ten right now. They all looked like how she felt—cold but pleased.

The McLeod Ganj movie halls had catholic tastes, Sabbah knew, since they primarily played DVDs the backpackers left behind. But this particular movie experience seemed like a hallucination. A few minutes into the slasher movie, something happened and they were swung into Vera Chytilova's *Daisies* instead. As Chytilova's girls ate and laughed and cheated fat businessmen and collapsed onto banquet tables, Sabbah revived.

At 1 a.m., she and the other patrons of the veggie shop cinema came up the metal staircase. She blinked into the light, not quite sober but relatively calm.

Walking slowly back to the hotel, she bumped into Rishi, whose well-fed vampire's face lit up at the sight of her.

'Hey, do you still want to go to Billing? The others ditched.'

She dimly recalled conversation about Bir and Billing, two villages a few hours from McLeod Ganj. For two months of the year, September and October, hang gliders from all over the world gravitated to these villages. Rishi and friends wanted to drive later that night to Billing and watch the early morning flights.

Her mood was sweetened by the comical anticipation of trotting out the bigot's defence on Twitter: I have many (insert community) friends. Now she too could say that she had a North Indian friend. But was Rishi really her friend? Perhaps she was too boring and too old to be his friend. She looked at him and brightened a bit. What did it matter? Tomorrow the trishuls may arrive.

There were few things that made her feel as glamorous as driving in the night. Expeditions in the night were affairs of urgency and pleasure. The very first time she was out at night was when, as a seven-year-old visiting an aunt's house outside Mangalore, she accompanied the teenage boys of the household to hunt frogs around the paddy fields. Wet, muddy and scared, she had never had as good a time as she had had then. Later, in an orchard closer home, the boys had cut the legs off and fried them precariously on a stolen pan. She had eaten the crunchy legs, looked at the slivers of sky between the trees and felt very worldly.

She looked at Rishi and wondered what kind of memories he had.

'Hush, little baby, don't say a word/Mama's gonna buy you a mockingbird,' sang Rishi under his breath. Her skin prickled as she looked sideways at him. Maybe Rishi was a serial killer. Maybe he would hit out with his left hand mid-syllable, knock her out, open her door, push her off the side of the mountain and continue on his way, singing about the diamond ring and billy goat Mama was gonna buy.

She looked out at the mountains, trembling slightly. In a while, Rishi broke the silence and began telling her stories. These stories were not gossip. They were stories about work. Stratagems, heroes, ambitions, late nights. 'I like my job,' he said with an ease that startled her.

Words had distinct history for Sabbah. The true meaning of some words only emerged after many years of knowing them. 'Irresistible' was once a favourite Robert Palmer video with a mass of identical women.

Right now, the word meant Rishi. Slack-jawed in repose, with clothes that fit too well and perfect hair, Rishi should have continued to spook her. Instead, she had to stop herself from grinning at him like a lunatic.

Do indeterminate North Indians have angst? What do they worry about? Who was this Rishi that he could befriend someone as uncool as her, and for no reason? How could she possibly waste her short life with self-doubt? She only had to make sure that she was never again in a room with more than two writers.

Utterly relaxed, she fell asleep.

BILLING

Sabbah woke up in a village. She was rarely pleased by this and resented sticking out like a sore thumb. But Bir was silent at dawn as they drove towards Billing.

They passed a temple, with a broad red ribbon tied to its top, and then a tree. Rishi gestured towards the temple.

'That's the Thermal Devi temple.'

'The what?'

'Billing is famous for its fantastic thermals. Hot air rising that helps the gliders. Best in the world. When you jump off Billing, you get the best thermals over the temple. The red ribbon is so that gliders can see the spot from the sky.'

She grinned a bit, cheered already by the prospect of more eccentricity.

And suddenly there they were in Billing, a small meadow, a few kilometres high in the sky, now covered with giant butterflies in various stages of furling and unfurling. Men in goggles—she could not see any women—were walking around in shiny lycra outfits and boots. She could hear half a dozen languages around her, and thick excitement in every language.

Rishi, of course, knew people. He waved to someone who showed them the best place to watch. This someone indicated to her that she ought to be jumping, not watching. But she was not listening. Human beings were leaping off high mountains—could you ever get used to that? She imagined sticking her toes out, arching her body and leaping into the sky. Perhaps Icarus was not as stupid as she'd imagined him when she was a moralising ten-year-old.

After an hour of watching, she turned around looking for Rishi, and was as startled as she had been by the hang gliders.

When had she started reading? She couldn't remember. She read in film festivals and at parties. She read in moving vehicles and in the shower, with one hand sticking out, holding the book dry. Why did she read? She couldn't remember.

Now this child was reading on the roof of the world when everyone around him was playing with their magnificent flying machines. In the morning, he looked less smooth than last night, but just as slack-jawed. He was staring almost cross-eyed at a book. His mug of coffee grew cold as he read. He read slowly. He turned pages with a finger the size of a little cucumber. She could not take her eyes away.

As she watched, her breathing slowed. The mountains disappeared around her. The world narrowed and focused on his slow reading. The way it used to when nothing in the world could get between her and a book.

What was he reading? She was afraid to find out. But it didn't matter. This morning, it was possible that she would die oxygen-starved as she surreptitiously watched his Neanderthal brow frowning at a book. After an eternity, he picked up his coffee and the book jacket swung into view. *A Room with a View*. Who'd have guessed? Rishi continued to read.

Twenty minutes later, she was still standing, disoriented, when Rishi was joined by three of his friends, all roughly in the same mould. Noisily they sank their heavy bodies and bags around him.

'What you reading?'

'Some shit,' replied Rishi, carefully marking his page with a folded corner before putting it away.

No Filter

Akansha and I once met a couple who thought they were in an open marriage. We'd lived on the same floor in Gurgaon for three years and visited each other's apartments three times in those three years. The fourth time we met, they told us that they were in an open marriage.

The man said they'd been married ten years and it was time to refresh the marriage. When he said 'refresh', I could only think of those warm, wet face towels you get in good salons. Then came the full waterfall of details, so many details. All the way down to who will screw outside the marriage on what day of the week. Tuesday evenings for her. Friday afternoons for him.

Akansha was a bit alarmed by this conversation with crazy strangers, I could see, but she did a good job of covering up. I wanted to ask them many questions, but after the answer to the very first one, I lost interest. I asked the man whether he or his square-shaped wife knew people who wanted to have sex with them? Neither did. This was just a fantasy, but they didn't know it was a fantasy. As if you could order love and sex like milk on an app. Idiots. People don't understand things. People don't understand people.

The next day at work I couldn't stop thinking about the poor idiots. They obviously did feel something unfathomable existed outside their boring marriage, but like dogs who sensed ghosts, they could only walk around in circles in the garden, barking. I stared at the hump of fat on the neck of the young developer who sat in front of me and felt sorry for the woman he was marrying. He had been meeting her at a different mall in Gurgaon every weekend ever since their engagement. Imagine having sex with him.

I, on the other hand, was as fit as the very last time Liji and I had been together. Much more actually. In all her Instagram pictures, Liji now had the cat-eyes style eyeliner. I liked it a lot. That was the only way in which she had really changed in all the years we had been separated. After a whole day of staring at that developer's neck hump for hours, I looked for my Liji on Facebook and found her. I pinged her for the first time in seven years.

Liji and I first reconnected on FB messenger, the world's most unromantic chat application. For several days we didn't shift to Whatsapp. We didn't discuss it but shifting felt like a decision with great implications. Once we did shift, within a few hours, I began to wish Akansha would go away and Sebastian would go away. If they would only leave and leave us alone.

We took many pictures in the backwaters on our first trip together after Akansha passed away. This was before I moved to Bangalore. I remembered right away to delete the photos from my phone after downloading them and hiding the files. I told Liji too. 'As if Sebastian would ever check,' she said.

I checked her Instagram regularly. Mostly there were just beautiful pictures of her. I couldn't bear to see her selfies with her idiotic husband, but she giggled when I asked her about them. 'We have selfies instead of sex, kutta. Don't be jealous.' Then she'd giggle more. Sebastian never saw those photos of us alone in a boat in still green waters, alone in the most beautiful landscape in the world—alone, except for the boatman. But later, the police did.

With the resort staff, Liji pretended she didn't understand Malayalam. I didn't want to come back to Kerala for the weekend, but Liji had insisted. I had thought she would say let's never go there again. In college, we couldn't wait to get out, get far away from the sticky, sweaty people pressing on us. Unexpectedly, in the water, I felt free, speaking Malayalam to the boatman and being ourselves.

When we were in the boat, I saw a tiny house on a handkerchief-sized island, an island just a few feet bigger than the house, and I asked Liji, 'Shall we come live here?'

She waved her hand at the water and the sky. 'Here? Without network?'

A little while later, we saw a woman on a boat rowing towards the tiny island. Her narrow boat had barely any space for her, stuffed as it was with cans of drinking water. Liji laughed at my expression.

───

I have always been very disciplined and honest, and that's why Akansha's father liked me so much. Those Delhi policemen would have liked to arrest me just like that, but the sight of a retired senior police officer standing up so strongly for his son-in-law made them think twice. If he said there was nothing suspicious in the way his daughter died, and she had slipped in the bathroom and cracked her head, what were they to say? They went away without looking too hard at anything. My father-in-law only cried and held my hand for a moment after they left. 'I had told her so many times to not leave oil on the bathroom floor. Always so careless, always.' I wondered whether he was imagining her slipping, or whether his brain was fried by the naked selfie he received from her phone just before she died. Well, technically after she died. Surely that must have been the last unforgiveable act of carelessness by his daughter as far as he was concerned.

It's true that Akansha was careless. Very intelligent but no follow-up. She never dried her hair properly after bathing and, in those Delhi parties with Punjabi girls and their perfectly straight hair, I used to get quite upset at the sight of her hair.

Her head had made a peculiar, soft crunching sound against the kettlebell. Perhaps it was true that there was nothing much in there, as her father had always joked. I couldn't believe the silliness of her having sex with the young Haryanvi boy in the flat next door. Fever. Didi took him khichdi. Then he took Didi to bed.

I was only guessing about the timing, but I was pretty sure her Florence Nightingale act must have been just a month before we got that open marriage lecture from our neighbours. Akansha hadn't made one peep while we were in their house. But when we left, she had laughed that rare, sharp laugh of hers, so at odds with her usual, vaguely worried expression. 'Why would anyone want an open marriage,' she said and laughed again. As if scared by that sound, a flock of tiny red birds rose from the tree next to our balcony. I looked them up later and eventually found their name: fire-capped tits.

A few weeks later, when Akansha and I were in the lift, I saw the Haryanvi boy and his Malayali flatmate, who had originally befriended us, exchange glances and smirk. In the mirror, I saw Akansha look down at the floor with such obviously fake disinterest that I knew. Liar, liar, tits on fire.

I knew and wanted to know more. I wanted to know so much more. I wished Akansha was Catholic and went to confession. I could have pretended to be the priest and hear everything.

Confession is not just in the movies, y'know. Back when we were young in Kerala, when we were together,

Liji used to go to confession in Catholic churches far from home and torment the priests. She used to tell them that she was newly married and that her evil husband was making her do all kinds of dirty, dirty things. The poor fellows used to try to make her feel better and tell her to cooperate with her husband. When she recounted those conversations, she'd howl with laughter. I'd shake my head and tell her that I was ready to convert to marry her, and she could continue doing this after we were married too. She laughed. Of course, then her father married her off to a readymade Catholic and I was left behind in the box, like the priest.

Eventually, my mother found Akansha on a matrimonial site and I said yes after our second meeting in a coffee shop in Gurgaon. Something about the curve of her full lips and her sad eyes made it easy to imagine a married life with her. One in which we would travel all over the world and speak in Malayalam to each other as we sat in the balconies of resorts, admiring the exotic views. Her mother was still alive back then, so I suppose she made sure her hair was combed properly the first few times.

I had more or less stopped thinking of Vinod. Except when I test-drove expensive cars.

Vinod and I had always loved fast cars. We'd spent hours and hours and hours looking at them online and watching races on TV before we got Internet. Vinod and I had been friends since KG. He was the first person I masturbated in front of and vice versa, I think. Vinod was the only person in the world who knew that when I masturbated I never ever thought of real women, the ones we saw on the streets or even in the movies. I could never satisfy myself in my fantasies unless I thought of the blonde, blue-eyed girls of my imagination. Ones who walked around in tiny denim shorts and white T-shirts that strained to contain their breasts.

After I figured out what my silly wife had been up to, after I'd reconnected with Liji, I test-drove six cars in two weeks. And every moment of those drives, despite the ridiculous chatter of the salesmen or the muscle power of the cars, I only thought of Vinod.

───

When I decided to dress up as a saffron-clad Haryanvi old man and video call Akansha, she needn't have answered the phone. She did. Why was she ready to believe that I was her Haryanvi lover's angry, religious uncle back home? Maybe my face was too well-disguised behind the grey beard I'd bought on Amazon. But she didn't recognise my voice, her own husband's voice. She really wasn't very bright. I didn't do video calls after that, but each time I called and berated her, I expected her to not pick up my call again. But she did and I insulted her again and she didn't protest. She heard me yell at her in Hindi, calling her a whore who had led my nephew astray and she didn't protest. When I told her I had seen the photos she had taken with my nephew, she didn't protest.

And then in my final phone call, one I made standing in the little park in our colony, I asked her to send me a naked picture. Send me a naked, smiling picture if she didn't want me to call her husband, I said to her, and she did. She was still half-dressed in the bathroom after sending that photo. I had to cover her up a little for the ambulance. After I used her fingers to forward the photo to her father.

So it shouldn't surprise you that, in Bangalore, I wondered whether I could try the same tactic on Sebastian. After all, if Akansha, who had looked like such a blameless woman, had been up to no good, surely it was possible that Sebastian was no saint either.

That vague hope is all I had. But I never imagined Sebastian would turn out to be such a huge fool! Or that he had been sleeping with prostitutes. Sebastian with his kanji personality. Sebastian who had had the unbelievable good luck to have been with my Liji for seven years. He disgusted me.

I had found it easy to befriend him in the lift until it swiftly reached a stage where we had keys to each other's houses. I had found it easy to pretend that Liji and I were strangers. After I found out what he was up to, for the first time since I had moved into their building in Bangalore, the acting became a true challenge.

Once, Sebastian invited me over to a meal with Liji's visiting parents, but I managed to extricate myself without stress. I didn't even feel the need to leave town. I didn't bump into Liji's parents in the building, but the possibility did not worry me. I was sure they would be as interested in pretending they didn't know me as I was.

When Liji was nineteen and her mother once found a pack of condoms in her handbag, she was ready to accept Liji's giggling explanation of a science project. As if we were sticking straws and matches and condoms on chart paper in engineering college. She just didn't want to know.

Another time, for many weeks, Liji and I wondered whether her father had seen us kissing at the bus stop in the rain. It was a little away from our area, so perhaps he didn't expect to see us there. Perhaps. The rain was warm in Kerala, not cold like it is in Bangalore.

I wonder how good my Haryanvi accent was when I had spoken to Akansha. Not bad, I suppose, since she had grown up in Delhi. As the imaginary Bishop of Bangalore, I just needed to put on the accents of one of those old-timer Malayalis who had gone to boarding school in Ooty. Much easier.

When I called him, Sebastian was disgusting and cried. He cried every time I called. Before the call, when he got the first mail from the bishop.net id I'd created, he must have peed in his pants. Just imagine getting a mail saying that the bishop had listened to the confessions of prostitutes and was concerned for you, a moral degenerate of a Malayali parishioner. Imagine believing that the bishop was emailing and calling personally to make you repent, sinner. Just imagine being a Catholic and believing all this. Sebastian and Akansha should have been married to each other. Same IQ and same morals.

Soon after I moved to Bangalore, I heard a song in a bar in Indiranagar. The singer asks his girlfriend about a man, a stranger who was aggressive to him. His girlfriend, like Akansha, had stared down at the ground. He keeps singing, 'Who is he and what is he to you?' I Shazamed it and heard it again and again. At one point, the song goes: you are too much for one man but not enough for two. Liji was too much for one man or even two, but I wanted her too-muchness, all of it.

I had hoped that I would make Sebastian confess to Liji that he had been cheating on her and manipulate him into leaving her alone. I had instructed Sebastian in my fourth bishop phone call to tell his wife the whole truth and offer her an out—a separation to allow her time to forgive him. It was either that or I would tell her myself, I told him. I had timed it so I could stand in the compound and see Sebastian sweating it out on the balcony. I could see his face crumpling as he hoarsely whispered into the phone that he would tell his wife that night, Father.

For a while in Bangalore, I was quite happy living next door to Liji and Sebastian. It was her Instagram feed that slowly made things difficult.

I woke up one morning and found a photo of Liji sleeping, beautiful in the light of their bedside lamp, a black lace nightie sliding just a little off her shoulder. I couldn't speak. The photo was so close to her face that I could see she had make-up on. I couldn't understand what kind of sick fuck would take photos of Liji like that and let her put it online where the whole world could see it. I almost brought it up with Sebastian. I was this close to asking him about it, but I still had self-control.

I knew my Liji and she liked dressing up and she was really going for it in Bangalore, unrestricted by who would see her, unrestricted by narrow-minded Malayalis.

She was having fun and I was all for it.

One day, she took me to a place in Indiranagar that had made customised bras for her. I didn't want to ask but hoped fervently that I could see her in it at the store. But when we got there, I could see from the saleswomen's faces that there was no chance they were going to let me into the changing room. One of the saleswomen gave me a rough estimate of what the bras were going to cost and I could only sigh. I mean, we were in India after all. What had I been thinking? Then the cubicle door opened and Liji stepped out in a silk robe. She smiled and parted her robe. She was dazzling in a brown-gold bra, the bra almost the same colour as her breasts, her shoulders, her collarbones, her stomach and the same colour as her panties. She smiled again and then took her warm kitten body back into the cubicle. The saleswomen and I all behaved as if nothing had happened. I paid and we left. On the way back to Koramangala, I stopped the car on the Ring Road and made her unbutton her shirt so I could stroke the ordinary bra she was wearing. She let me stroke her with a ghost of the smile from the store.

I only saw that gold bra again when we went to Goa and I took pictures of her on the lounger in the balcony, robe parted, a kitten in the sun.

But the Instagram pictures that Sebastian took of her every day, in new clothes every week, those I found near unbearable. One night, they went to a Halloween party in his office and he took photos of her dressed as a tiger. I could see everything, just everything in those photos. He had turned Liji into a performing animal.

Vinod and I had been lucky enough to get into the same engineering college. Then he got engaged in his second year. Arranged marriage! Around the same time, I met a fascinating junior called Liji Samuel.

Vinod didn't like Liji, I knew though he never said anything. And Liji had no interest in Vinod. That balance—of my twin pillars who wanted nothing to do with each other—worked in the beginning. Later, the roof came crashing down.

When I stole my mother's diamond earrings, my father thrashed her, assuming she had sold it to buy more of her precious orchid cuttings. Not that he would have forgiven her even if she had sold it to save me on my deathbed. Vinod didn't have much to say about the drama playing out in my house though he could probably hear it three houses down. Then, after a college play, we were waiting in the wings wearing big moustaches and golden armour. The girls (the real girls, not the pretend girls in our cast) returned to the wings after singing the college song. In the gloom, he saw the diamond earrings Liji was wearing. He saw and knew. Above his fake moustache, his eyes swung to me with a disgust I had never seen even when I had eaten snot in front of him. Who is she? And what is she to you?

Liji and I went to Nandi Hills when Sebastian was away in Bombay. The most boring trip on earth. Not a thing to see and the most aggressive monkeys. We left thirty minutes after arriving. When we were driving back down to Bangalore, I drove fast and we both cheered up. Liji leant into me, as close as she could despite the gearbox. She put her hand on my knee and crept it higher as I drove faster. We passed a battered car driving up the hill much, much faster than us and I caught an unforgettable glimpse of the driver through the window. His shirt and his gaunt face and his too-long hair and the elbow stuck out of the window on that summer day. Not AC-and-closed-windows like every other car. He was a villain from a Seventies movie trying to get away from a crime scene. Perhaps the police were driving uphill with sirens blaring.

Perhaps he was a time traveller, the body was back in the Seventies and he had been driving up Nandi Hills trying to get away from the pool of blood on the bathroom floor. Like someone who had pushed a boy into a waterfall on an impulse and wished he hadn't needed to.

Liji, who has always known the exact moment my mind wandered away from her, squeezed slightly at my thigh and I was back in the present. I smiled at her and I wished I had a convertible.

Of course there was no option of getting angry with Liji. It was just not on the menu. Liji always knew what I was feeling. She knew it weeks before I felt it. She also knew when I was resentful that she knew what I was feeling. When she had called me in my first year in Delhi to tell me she was getting married to a man her father had picked, I knew then too that there was nothing I could say. And nothing to say now. Of course, despite the suffering, it was right that we hadn't tried to get married back then. She had to send me out in the world to make my own way. I knew that.

But the morning after I had instructed Sebastian to confess all to Liji, I couldn't be my usual reasonable self. I couldn't understand what Liji was doing. I had created a perfect, clean opportunity for us. She just had to be righteously angry and throw him out of her house and her life for cheating on her with whores.

I managed to lie quietly in bed that Sunday morning. I didn't open Whatsapp. There was no point. She wasn't going to message me as soon as it happened. I had to be patient. I did push-ups. I bathed. I drank my protein shake. By noon I was coming out of my skin. I scrolled down Instagram aimlessly and then felt like a truck had hit me. On Liji's Instagram account there were pictures from early that morning in the courtyard of St Francis Xavier's Cathedral and then photos of brunch at The Park. Had he not told her? No, he was too scared to defy the bishop. He had somehow told her and then what happened?

I made myself wait another hour and then I called Sebastian from the bishop number. It was hard to school my voice into even a remote semblance of the overly intrusive old priest I had easily pulled off before. I was so keen to ask him straight, 'Why hasn't she dumped your ass?' Sebastian was once more disgusting and his voice broke as he told me that Liji had forgiven him and he would never stray again. I wanted to curse him violently in Malayalam. My vision grew dark and I thought I would faint. I wanted to call Liji and scream into the phone. I made myself sit down. Liji and I would never be together if I lost control. She would have nothing to do with me if I lost control.

Since I didn't do a video call eventually, it turned out I didn't need to dress up as the bishop, but while I was still thinking my plans through, I had gone to a cavernous costume shop in Ulsoor. I tried on a few beards. Then I tried a few crowns. Then beards and crowns. Around me, small girls and their mothers were renting up great piles of Bharatanatyam gear, weighing the fake plaits and seeing if they were too heavy for their small heads.

Eventually, the salesmen fished out a Catholic priest's costume I'd asked for, but it was too small for me. My chest and arms would not have fit the costume even before I started lifting seriously. I remembered the smell of the gym that Vinod and I used to go to when I had first decided I wanted muscles like him. I remembered also the smell of the make-up we wore for plays. We did so many through school and college. Dressed as kings, soldiers, old men, young women. Vinod was often cast as a woman in our boys' school and in engineering college. Because he was so willing to play anything, no one remembered that he was so tall and burly. Somehow he could make himself a breathy, curvy woman that everyone wanted to take pictures with afterwards. 'What is the secret of your success as a woman?' one of our college classmates once asked him, his fist held up like a TV reporter's microphone. 'The secret of my success *as* a woman is…my success *with* women,' said Vinod. Those fools would have laughed at anything Vinod said. In the explosion of laughter that followed, only I heard him say, 'The secret of my success *as* a woman is my success with women's secrets.'

The week before I made the bomb call, I went to the lake near my office and tried to SWOT our present and visualise our future. I had tried to visualise it at my desk earlier. I focused and worked at it, but our future never became a clear photo. This exercise had worked for my career at every stage, but it was failing me now. I thought hard of a nice, casual Instagram post in our future. A photo in which Liji and I were laughing and playing in the waves in our swimsuits. It still didn't come together. I went to the office gym. I gave up in ten minutes. That's when I went to the lake to walk and smoke even though I hadn't had a cigarette in years. Before I could even light up, I saw a red flash in the corner of my eye. A tiny red bird flew by. It wasn't the same but reminded me a little of the flock I had seen in Gurgaon before Akansha had died. And then I knew what to do. Liji and I needed Sebastian out of the picture. The bishop had not worked out. And no policeman father-in-law would be around to defend Liji, so his departure would have to be a bloodless and blameless one.

The next time I came down to the lake, my plans were solid. I had smuggled the ID documents from Sebastian's house to get the new SIM. Everything was in place. I had to pick the right moment and three planes would be grounded after my call. Vans full of cops would approach Sebastian's office as I sat far away in my own. He would be arrested as a terrorist or something.

It had rained the previous night and so I couldn't stay long at the lake, I knew. This lake was going to do its infamous thing in a few hours and turn into a foaming hellhole. Then passers-by could expect to be hit by great, stinking chunks of foam. It could even catch fire as it did once a year. I didn't intend to hang out that long. My plans were solid. No chance of seeing the red bird again.

I looked at the water for a while and, as I was walking back, I sensed some movement at the edge of my vision. I swung around at high speed. I thought I could smell Vinod. Vinod as he used to smell, smoky and masculine, not bloated and rotting as he was when they fished him out of the water three days after he was lost at the excursion. It was much harder to pull him out than to push him in.

We were careful about spending time together in the building, but one day she came across the courtyard to my flat and I spent the whole afternoon biting her back. From the back of her neck to the dimples at the bottom of her spine. She kept giggling.

In college, when we used to take the bus together, she had once signalled to me that I should bite the woman standing next to us. Liji made kathakali eyes towards the curve of the woman's waist in her sari and tiny biting gestures with her sharp, tiny teeth. I didn't think or worry about who would see me in that crowded bus. I leant across Liji to the woman in the aisle. For what seemed like an endless moment, I was enveloped by the smells of both women. The soft edge of the woman's sari brushed my face and I could smell soap and powder coming off her stomach. On the left side of my body, I could smell Liji—floral with an underlying feral, animal stink that I always wanted to drown in. For a moment I thought I'd faint. I quickly nipped the woman at the waist and withdrew in a flash. She squealed and looked down and only saw Liji sitting calmly next to her. I was looking out of the window.

When we were together, we could do anything. We were never afraid. Liji was never afraid.

Very occasionally, I wished I could rely on Liji to just do what I wanted her to do. When I had told Akansha what I wanted, it got done. Looking at Liji's calm, open face, no one would guess that she had any secrets at all. She wouldn't be nervously sleeping with some boy in the same building and hiding it from me. But here she was, taking that calm, open face and going on holiday with her cheating husband and ready to have sex with him.

'I don't want you to go to Bali with him.'

'Why?'

'You know why.'

She looked at me over her shoulder with her pleasant, clear gaze and all the reasons I knew she shouldn't go to Bali dried up in my mouth.

'He is my husband and we are going to Bali.' She flicked her hair aside giving me clearer access to her back.

Ever since I had heard about the Bali plans, I had been unable to sleep. I looked up the resort Sebastian had booked and saw that a major attraction was the Bali Swing. It was all over Insta. Liji hadn't said, but I knew she would definitely try the high swing and fly into the air laughing into the view of the river. And that piece-of-shit Sebastian would be there to take her photos for Insta. It's the #baliswing hashtag that had made them decide to book in the first place, I found out later. What else could he do for her?

I imagined Liji swinging in a long silk pavada with white jasmine in her hair, an outfit I'd seen her in only once for a college dance.

Breaking all the rules of our love, I stuttered to her, 'He wants to keep us apart.'

Liji looked over her shoulder at me. 'Of course he does. Everyone wants to separate us.'

Hearing her agree was the first thing that calmed me down. I bit her left shoulder gently. Her flesh was so soft it felt like, if I bit hard enough, my teeth would pierce through all the way to her heart.

⁂

Of all my performances, I feel like my call to the airport was the worst. I dressed up quite a bit for no reason and headed out on the road to the airport. And in Devanahalli I made the call with the new number I had registered to Sebastian. One number no one picked up. For the longest time. Then I got put onto an IVR and, for some reason, I accidentally kept picking Kannada choices. It took me twenty minutes to finally get to a human. By then I was sweating and angry. I had almost become Sebastian. I forgot my dialogue when the squeaky female voice finally answered and I mumbled that there were bombs on three flights. I rattled off the flight numbers and cut the call. In my rage at myself, I called Liji to complain. When she answered the phone, I said, Hi.

'What number is this,' she asked sharply.

'Forget that. I just wanted to tell you.'

'What?'

'That you don't need to pack for Bali.'

'What are you talking about?'

'Never mind.'

I calmed down just with that short exchange, just from hearing her voice and remembering why I was doing all this. I hung up and immediately removed the SIM from the phone and cut it in two. Then four. Then I drove away, a small part of my mind on what it would be like to drive that stretch in a dark blue Mercedes convertible.

Even as fiercely chaperoned as our college group was at the waterfalls, we hadn't been the only couple to sneak some time alone. When Vinod saw us emerging from the shrubs, his eyes flickered over our bodies. And I saw his gaze slow down over Liji's face. Even through the delirium that affected me every time Liji and I touched each other, I saw. I saw her eyes flash at him like the earrings had in the dark.

How could I not have realised or remembered that of course Sebastian's own phone would show that he had been sitting in his office, quietly thinking about money, when the bomb calls had been made?

Of course, of course, if I am going to be honest, it must have been that moment of loss of control when I panicked and called Liji for reassurance that really got the police suspicious. If Sebastian, the man who owned the bomb hoax phone, hadn't made the call, and whoever did make the call had called Sebastian's wife, I mean naturally they would have been suspicious. I am not sure how they decided it was me. Perhaps they saw that my own phone had been near Devanahalli when the call had been made.

Akansha's father had wanted to help his poor son-in-law falsely accused of terrorism. He had flown down from Delhi and was helpful until the moment late at night when that particular piece of information about the call to Liji had drifted like a curl of smoke through the surprisingly big and airy police station. I saw the moment it reached him, across the room from where I was cuffed to a wooden chair. I saw his wide face and thick neck turning grey.

I will see Liji again even though right now she has to

tell everyone that she doesn't know anything. What else is she going to say while I am sitting in jail?

I have to trust Liji. Every time she came into my life, she has set challenges before me and I have risen to them. It was the only way I could have escaped becoming another loser back home. I have to trust Liji and eventually I will see her again. And no one will separate us when we take selfies as we swing into the sky in Bali.

The Singer and the Prince

How did the singer meet the prince? In all stories of love, we must know how the lovers met, how they met again, how they almost missed each other and, sometimes, how they never met.

The singer and the prince should have had a chorus in the background when they first met. At the very least, they should have had a fight. Her scooter hits his cycle. His cycle hits her horse cart. They don't have *misomeru* (the feeling on first meeting that this is just the person you've been looking for), but eventually, in hindsight, they would say they had *koi no yokan* (the feeling on first meeting that this is going to tumble into love). How does one manage vehicular collision on the internet, and why would the prince and the singer have Japanese feelings? But this is not my story, so you don't have to listen to me rambling on about what I want.

ABOUT THE SINGER

Small-town women who run away to the city are like the Powerpuff Girls, with cute, overly feminine clothes and superpowers. The singer was a small-town girl who had ambled citywards with her mother and stayed in Bangalore till no one knew that her past contained ten-kilometre walks to school.

She was a big woman with big eyes, wild hair and great mounds of soft flesh. She did not think of herself as fat, and hence funny. She rarely poked jokes at her own abundance and was startled when others did, expecting her to be cool. When they saw her astonished expression, they cringed and rarely ribbed her again. Men were ashamed of how badly they wanted to nuzzle her and how much they wanted to fuck her some afternoons. They plotted ways of enjoying her in secret, like a box of unfashionable sweets. Women who were not very perceptive said in admiring tones that the singer was very comfortable in her body.

The truth was that, for most of her life, the singer had never spent any time thinking of her body. Until one day, oh cursed day. Rushing past a shiny surface on Commercial Street, she caught sight of her reflection and was frozen by the thought that this was what other people saw. On her scooter, she didn't sing much that day. What if she'd been small and thin like other Kannadiga girls, with soft brown eyes and fragile shoulders? Or tall and thin? Or a man? Or had no body at all? Wouldn't it have been wonderful if people were just minds? And voices, of course, voices. The singer's own voice shook badly built houses and well-protected hearts, but when small men saw where the voice came from, they quailed, shivered, smiled lopsided smiles and talked loudly. Small-town girls have x-ray vision that makes the scaffolding of pretence visible. She did not sigh, but she did despair at ever falling in love.

HOW THEY MET

She took on very few students and found most of them tiresome. One of them, a girl who could sense light from dark but could see no more than that, also had the tendency to fall in love with someone new every few months. The blind girl met her lovers at her numerous musical lessons scattered across the city. A madrigal singer here, a cellist there and a mridangam artiste in Malleswaram. One weekend, she dragged the singer to show her the newest object of her affections, the lead singer of a rock band. After the gig at a small, noisy Brigade Road pub, he came by and said hello to the student. The singer watched with interest as her student arched towards his smoky Austin Town Tamil-accented voice. Unlike the teacher, the student could not see the kindly but slightly puzzled expression on the man's face. The student was in love with him for some months before she moved to the scratchy timbre of a jazz pianist who had just moved to Cox Town.

One day, the student announced that she was in love with a lovely man, a music engineer from the US, and that she was meeting him for the first time this weekend. First time? The singer was told that the student's newest pool of kindly musical men had been found on the internet. The music engineer and she had met online and been chatting for weeks. He was coming home on holiday and was dying to meet her.

When was the last time the singer had had sex? She couldn't remember. Meanwhile, little chits like her student, who had strong feelings about guarding their virginity, were meeting men all the time. The net, was it? The singer had left her small town and come to Bangalore with no worries about fitting in. She took to the internet without fear and without expectations.

She found lots of music chat rooms and was at first desperately bored. Offline, she had always behaved as if her classical training was only good for stories of folly and pretension. She had eschewed performing in the katcheri circuit altogether a long time ago, unwilling to genuflect that much every day. Occasionally, she went to a concert when she suspected the performer may not live to do another show. She professed a great love for old Bollywood instead. But the heart is not egalitarian. This was 2003 and most chatrooms were filled with men whose 'favourite singer' was A.R. Rahman. Rather swiftly, she fled, looking for the classical music chatrooms, where she was puzzled to discover that everyone was worried about Indian culture; and the men specifically wanted her photo with Indian culture or wanted her photo without Indian culture.

The singer told none of her friends about how she walked fast and guiltily through these rooms, hoping for a kindred soul. Someone for whom the music in his head made the world less banal, as it did for her. Someone who had a body but would not see hers. After a while, she began picking fights with the men she met in these chatrooms and they either skittered away or stayed on to fight peevishly.

To all women in search of a story, there eventually must come a prince. Across a crowded chatroom, their eyes met.

prince_nakshatram: How can you say that my guru is terrible? He is wonderful.

thumri_girl: *Pyare rasiya bihari, suniyo arz hamari.*

prince_nakshatram: Lol. I've not heard that one for a long long time. Bade Ghulam Ali?

thumri_girl: Full marks but I insist that your guru's voice is too nasal.

prince_nakshatram: Fellow!!! He is a gem of a person and a great musician.

thumri_girl: Gem-kyem, I don't know. That nasal voice!

prince_nakshatram: In classical music, 'what' is important, not 'how'.

thumri_girl: Please saaar! I've heard those stories before. Don't give me lecture and think that I won't notice terrible voices.

For a few days they typed violently and musically at each other, paused and sat back, only to type some more. Then her mobile phone rang and the prince had a voice.

VOICE TO VOICE, LIP TO LIP

thumri_girl: God bless Skype.

prince_nakshatram: God bless Skype.

The prince and the singer blessed Skype many times over the next few months. The singer was newly capable of flirtation. She was Gargi, she was Maitreyi, but she had oomph. She continued to criticise his favourite musicians. He only laughed and stayed to argue and sing at her, addressing her as if she was a drawing room audience in Dharwad.

Eventually, she could not resist telling her friends about her nocturnal adventures between the Indian and Austrian time zones. Friends of lovers usually introduce unwelcome prosaic notes, but in this case, the element I introduced was one that heightened the drama. I told the singer kindly that, from the clues he'd been dropping in their chats and conversations, he most probably was a real prince.

Me: Have you Googled him?

thumri_girl: Shut up!

Me: Then I'll do it for you.

Despite her protestations, the prince was Googled and unmasked. It hadn't been much of a mask, anyway, just one of those that elegantly reveal the nose and manly jawline, leaving only silly girls in doubt of his identity.

thumri_girl: You didn't tell me, da.

prince_nakshatram: I'm sorry. It's nice to be here and talk music with someone not from the concert circuit, someone who doesn't know me, my gurus, my uncles and my mother.

I reminded the singer that royalty had a reputation for wandering incognito, usually on quests to win a prize or gain wisdom from new experiences, but she didn't really need such an explanation. The singer was kind and railed against neither fat nor fact.

HOW THEY MET AGAIN

The singer cannot be imagined without her blue Kinetic Honda. On this scooter she ran errands for her mother, who sculpted gods out of granite. Her mother was just as likely to send her to argue with a pious client about the size of a statue as she was to send her to fetch vegetables.

A long time ago, on this scooter she rode to a katcheri organised by Hindu fundoos. She was close to quitting even then but didn't want to miss a chance to sing thumris composed by her Muslim guru, her first guru, the one whom she'd left as a teenager and whose own guru's tomb in Gujarat was festooned with burning tires a few years ago. On this scooter she rode to the hospital early one morning to look at the corpse of a friend who'd hung herself while her two lovers quarrelled outside. On this scooter she rode to rescues and consolations, to cigarettes and coffee and upma.

Her scooter is what she missed the most when she went to the prince's Kerala palace to study his music. Every time she wanted to pee, he drove her to the nearest

Taj hotel. It does not matter that you are Brahmin, he told her. To my family, you are an outsider who should only use the servants' bathrooms. She sat impassive and grand in the passenger seat of the old Mercedes and fantasised about riding up to the palace on her blue scooter, parking it in the driveway and walking in with her helmet in her left hand.

She had imagined that the palace would be on higher ground, with a driveway that began with lions on top of pillars. She had imagined there would be sentries in livery. Instead, there had been three tall men in safari suits and quiet moustaches.

The prince had taught her three words to say to these men who guarded the palace from commoners and garlic. She should say, 'Thampuran. Pattu. Padikyan.' 'His Highness. Song. Study.' The guards had fallen about laughing and sent for someone to take her inside. The singer thought of the television show about Mrignayanee, the Gujjar girl Maharaja Man Singh Tomar had met while out hunting. He'd fallen in love with her when he saw her separate two buffaloes, horns locked in combat, with her bare hands. Walking through the palace, the singer felt like Mrignayanee must have when she thought it would be okay to appear in her traditional clothes in the royal court.

Did Man Singh and Mrignayanee have a threesome with their guru Baiju Bawra, the singer thought distractedly as she was escorted into the presence of the prince. The prince was drinking tea.

Fleshmeet is the technical term, she thought as he stood up to greet her. Meat. There was no doubt that the prince was a substantial man, much bigger than his font size. A man who matched his voice, had no nervous tics or fluttering fingers. Her mind flew to her first guru, a tiny, skinny, grinning man from Dharwad who smoked cigarette after cigarette, sitting cross-legged on any available flat surface. He had always looked less like a legendary ustad with diamond-hard standards than like the man who hands you bananas and milk at the corner shop.

The prince and the singer had a five-day musical interlude before she went back to Bangalore and he flew to Salzburg.

A month later, he sent her a tiny white gift.
Ride a cockhorse to this iPod cross
And see my fine lady ride on a white horse.
Rings on her fingers and bells on her toes
She shall have music wherever she goes.

The singer was ecstatic. She couldn't understand when she had stopped listening to music. She couldn't understand how she had not had this before. She couldn't understand how the universe had made it possible for all its musicians to sit lightly on her shoulder, hang nimbly from her earlobes and sing. She was sitting in Cubbon Park. Two men masturbated sporadically in front of her for two hours. The sun crossed the sky and policemen came to frighten decent women home. She didn't move, didn't shift, didn't squirm on the concrete bench.

She rode home that night without the music playing in her ears. She smiled when bus horns shrieked and trumpeted. That night in her dreams the prince was a giant straddling continents. A week later, her friends were startled to hear that the singer had consented to sing, had herself organised a small concert in someone's living room.

'Really? *Really*?' they asked each other and, more carefully, her. Really? Perhaps she would finally give up the job where she told people from Millersville and Beavers Fall and Middlebury what their credit limits were. She didn't, but several small living room congregations over the next year clutched their hearts when she sang.

WHY SHE HAD LEFT

A year passed. The prince returned and they met at the palace again to sing to each other. One evening at the Taj, post outcaste-tinkle, they drank bad coffee. Mid-conversation, he clapped her on the shoulder. The singer sighed. It was the death knell of romance, she knew. So the conversation that followed didn't surprise her as much as it should have.

'Why are you so crass, man?' the prince asked.

'Crass? What is crass?' Like many other people, the singer only knew as many words in English as she needed to know.

The prince waved his soft hands. 'Crass means rude. Low class.' Now the prince cringed as he heard the words coming out of his mouth. 'You smoke all the time.

You hardly sleep. You do these random performances for people who don't know anything about Hindustani music. You don't believe in morning riyaz. It's because you've left serious music behind and begun working among these uncultured BPO types.'

The singer laughed. 'Even Gangubai needed to pay the bills and feed her children.'

'But Gangubai did it through music!' he protested.

Let me tell you a story, she said.

The singer told the prince many stories that day. But the first one was enough. When she was twenty-two and keenly studying music with her second guru, she attended concerts feverishly. Not a syllable was sung in Bangalore without her hearing it. For the bigger concerts, she would beg ticket favours, sneak in, stand in the aisles, try to plaster herself to the walls. And as her face became better known, smaller organisers who needed bums on seats would call her and her best friend. Those days, the singer liked being liked and broke no rules. She touched the feet of elders, washed her guru's clothes, ran his errands and kept her mouth shut and smiling.

The story begins on an evening when the marquee event was a husband-and-wife duo—brilliant vocalists legendary for their joint performances. Marquee being a loose description when the event was unadvertised, organised at a time of day when only the truly unemployed could attend and held in a Malleswaram high school.

Ten minutes before the event came the news that the accompanist was stuck in a traffic jam. The singer was asked if she would accompany the couple on the tanpura. This turned out to be an unfortunate vantage position. The couple, seated close to each other and smiling at the genteel audience, was surreptitiously and violently pinching and clawing each other even as they sang the ragas newspapers always described as 'mellifluous'. Each wanted the other one's voice to halt so their own could fly out and wrap itself around the solid mass of attendant Kanjeevaram sarees. Afterwards, watching the pair put on ethereal airs, she knew she could never listen to them again. It was the first of many incidents that led her to the safe, anaemic BPO where she worked.

Having told her stories and made the prince laugh, she also saw for the first time how embarrassed the prince was by any unpleasantness, by crassness. She was convinced she'd always be his 'bold' and 'unusual' friend, not an object of romance. Her terracotta heart now had a hairline crack. He didn't love her. He didn't want her. This was as clear to her as if he had typed it out for her.

Another year passed. The prince visited her many times and they met in Bangalore coffee shops. She visited the palace again. On one visit, she casually greeted a wraith in the corridor, but it glared at her and glided away. 'That was my mother, the Maharani!' the shocked prince told her. 'No one just says hello to her.' The singer was unimpressed. The previous weekend at home, she had heard loud laughter and gone out into the courtyard. Her old mother was sitting astride the granite shoulder of her new Vishwamitra and waving her chisel in the air.

'Look, kanna, I've done such a bad job. He looks like that chief minister after he had the stroke. The Saptarishi Ashram will never hire me again!' What is a mere queen after that?

The prince was as admiring of the singer as if she had separated fighting buffaloes. He told her of his fear and hate of the hard women of his household, who bullied him and decided what he should eat and how he should eat it. Only his music was left alone, entrusted in the hands of his soft-bellied gurus. He likes me because I'm too big to be a woman, she thought.

I dismissed this line of thought. I told her that King Cophetua was never interested in women, he was only interested in feeling good about himself. I said it to console her. King who? she asked. Famous fairy tale. There was a king. One day he saw a beggar girl, fell in love with her and raised her to be his queen. Cophetua: the singer rolled the name around in her mouth.

THE BEAUTY

The drawing room concerts continued—sometimes shattering furniture to kindling and sometimes not. Sometime that year, on an off-day, she looked about on Orkut for music lovers and found them still fixated on A.R. Rahman and Jagjit Singh. She was thinking of deleting her account when she discovered a fake Jagjit Singh having an uproarious fight with a fake Lata Mangeshkar. She stayed in the peanut gallery and enjoyed herself.

The singer smoked much more now, something she learnt to do stylishly among the hijras whose company she'd wandered into. She had met Soundarya at a dark bus stop where she was hustling languidly. The singer found her funny and sweet and took to hanging out with her friends, and on rare occasions, at the Ulsoor hamam, where Soundarya and her guru lived in a state of constant negotiation. Could Soundarya wear pants? Occasionally, and far from the hamam, her guru relented after weeks of Soundarya's teasing and arguing.

'I think I'll buy myself a denim mini-skirt,' Soundarya responded.

The guru roared, 'You're so lucky I'm not chucking you out, as my guru would have!'

Soundarya said the equivalent of whatevz and merrily continued to scandalise her sari-wearing, flower-festooned sisters. Generation gap, the older hijra complained to the singer.

With Soundarya and in the hamaam, the singer felt at home, both warmly accepted and a sexual object, as if this wasn't like trying to pat your stomach and rub your head at the same time. Still, when she took Soundarya to meet the prince, it was a slightly malicious gesture. The prince had come to Bangalore to see her and, as usual, to persuade her that she must return to serious music before it was too late. And certainly she shouldn't ride about in the night on her scooter, smoking cigarettes and killing her voice.

She secretly hoped that the prince would smell the

street and dark corners and unpleasant evenings on Soundarya and be frightened by how much his friend had moved away from respectability and the starched katcheri circuit. Even her unflappable mother had been startled at the news of these recent friendships. But with the first few syllables of introduction, she knew she had cut off her nose to spite her face. She didn't delude herself by thinking that he would run when he discovered that Soundarya was not a woman. The prince had fallen in love.

Over the next week, the singer barely saw him, and always, with Soundarya. Room service, running water and thick towels had given Soundarya a serenity last bestowed on Julia Roberts. Her hoarse, gentle, sexy voice was barely audible as it whispered and rasped near the prince's ears.

Both Soundarya and the prince had moved beyond the singer, leaving her in the land of the crass and unlovable.

Soon the prince made arrangements for Soundarya to go to Salzburg with him. With extreme reluctance, she wore shirt-pants and cut her hair and was passport-photo'ed into sullen Santosh Siddalingiah.

The singer's friends watched to see if she would fade away in heartbreak, but she stayed whole as the marble, founded as the rock. With the appalling insensitivity of new jubilant lovers, the prince had told her before he left, 'If you don't start practising seriously, you'll lose your voice. I'm not sure whether it hasn't been damaged already from neglect.' The singer bit back her desire to hit him and to tell him that his mother would stew him in garlic when she found out about Soundarya.

THE FUNERAL

Now the emails from Austria came with photos. They talked a lot on Skype since the couple wanted her to hear their happiness, not just see them in winterwear. Besides, Soundarya, her lovely, warm friend, who would have been the more entertaining correspondent, could barely write in English. The singer grimly replied to these emails with many smileys (as she did to the ones from her former student who had flown to the US with her music-engineer boyfriend. The girl had said that it was better to be blind in America than sighted in India).

In every email, the prince urged the singer to perform more and to bigger audiences. Take on more students. They'll pay your bills. Give up the bloody call centre. It's ruining your voice.

The singer was on the verge of ending the annoying correspondence for good when the 'Mother serious' mail arrived. This subject line was obviously Soundarya's idea of humour, because the prince himself was devastated. The family had found out, arrived in Salzburg and ordered the prince to break all ties with this 'freak'. They'd threatened Soundarya, bribed her, been cold to her, attempted to disrobe her, and tried all the other tactics known to angry royalty down the ages. Soundarya walked away, naked and amused, to sun herself on the small Viennese balcony. The family returned home and organised a ritual to declare the prince dead.

Later, on her webcam, the singer saw the prince clutch his soft, straight hair and say, 'Padi adachu, pindam vacchu. They shut their doors and conducted my funeral. I'm not sure if even my gurus will talk to me.'

The singer gave up her initial schadenfreude and set about applying her fine common sense to the situation.

Small-town girls have superpowers. She convinced the prince that the family would die before telling anyone he was in love with a hijra. The funeral was to frighten him into returning home, and then they'd declare him undead. If he felt like going home, he could go without Soundarya. It was not the end of the world. Or he could take her home with him and find out if it really was.

How would his half-blind ninety-year-old guru in Chennai guess Soundarya was a hijra? And if he did, maybe he wouldn't act like the royals? And what about Bal Gandharva? What about him, the prince wanted to know. The singer had to admit here that she'd just thrown in Bal Gandharva without thinking it through, but the rest of the stuff she knew for sure. The prince had to be a grown-up now and stop whining at his amma.

For weeks she wrote dozens of emails trying to cheer him up and stiffen his backbone. One of her subject lines was: To the artiste formerly known as Prince. I'd ventured this joke, explained it to the singer and it had amused her a great deal. Finally, her ceaseless emails seemed to work.

He made a quick visit to the palace without Soundarya. His mother refused to see him, but he threatened the rest of the family with dire things if they didn't lay off the drama. Such as? Such as sending his wedding photos to the press. Such as getting married to Soundarya. It's allowed in Austria, you know, sort of, he blustered to the blanched family. He flew back trembling.

The singer said as cheerily as she could on Skype, 'I didn't know you had it in you.' Soundarya guffawed peering into the screen, 'Neither did I.'

The prince was slowly restored to his expansive self, urging her to do riyaz more often. She was careful not to tell him that she had given notice at the BPO. She didn't want him to have any more ammunition.

She bought a new scooter with her last full-time salary from the call centre. What was a girl to do with this free time? She rarely had the old impulse now to ride wildly through the flower stalls, singing loudly, scattering Russell Market before her. She didn't blame the scooter. Though she did periodically wish it was as dented and dusty as her old one. This new thing seemed alien to her shabby self.

Three months later, the scooter was slightly less shiny. One night, the singer went into the bathroom for a shower. A chisel lay on the counter where her mother had abandoned it. She picked it up. Absentmindedly, she stood on the cold floor, flexing her arm and enjoying its weight. She held it over her right breast. Imagine cutting your flesh off. She contemplated the cool, horizontal line of the blade pressing into her skin. And suddenly her hand trembled with the effort of not cutting herself.

She might have wept, her once-a-year crying jag, when she heard her mother's fat laughter from the dim courtyard. The singer looked out of the bathroom window and saw that her mother, in response to the urgent and prudish desires of her clients, was painting a pale pink loincloth over a plaster-of-paris sadhu's crotch. Spotting her face at the window, her mother waved.

The singer giggled, ate two badams to improve her memory and went to bed. The next morning she woke at 5 a.m. and sang.

Missed Call

Last night two squabbling cats leapt on to my son's chest. They bounced out of the corridor and landed in the dark on Vijay, who was sleeping with his head in the room and the rest of his body in the corridor. He nearly shat from fear and was actually burning with fever by the morning. I told him to stay home from school, but also couldn't help ragging him a bit. He's very tall now, nearly six feet, and working at a gym after school so that he can body-banao for free. He didn't fancy my teasing him at all.

It doesn't help that his younger brother is scared of no living creature, and is constantly catching scorpions and strange insects and making kissy noises at the baby shark that's growing at an alarming speed inside our fish tank. The fish tank, too, has grown at an alarming pace in the house. At first we had the little one that Ritu Madam had given us when she left Delhi and moved to a Pune school. Manu was six then. Some of the staff had looked peculiarly at her, no doubt thinking, 'Do you really need to give the cafeteria cook who lives in some slum a fish tank?' But Ritu Madam understood Manu even then. Today, the fish tank is almost a third of the room. When we bought our TV, it had to be a size and shape that would allow space for future baby sharks or whatever other godforsaken creature Manu would bring home.

Manu himself wouldn't have teased his elder brother about the cats. It's just Vijay's pride that's a bit hurt. In these last six months, he has grown into thinking of himself as a man. He's almost sixteen. Vijay told me in as many words when I had my accident: 'Now, Ma, you be our child for a while.' No one knows that, in the first month after the accident, he had to wipe me down, help me walk across the corridor to the loo and steady me as I squatted. He even washed my blood-stained underwear for a week. Funny now that I think of it. Radha, who went to work at the parlour, even the day after my accident, never thought to ask how I managed all day. She must have thought it was a good thing her brothers were home from school to help me and left it at that.

Everyone in Begumpur told me, 'You're so lucky that, when the car hit you, the driver stopped. Who takes responsibility these days? Who takes someone to hospital and pays for all the treatment?' I never disagreed, never let on that I didn't feel grateful for two broken collarbones and a cracked hip, though I did feel grateful for my good, smart children who took care of me. I kept smiling as I had smiled a few years ago when people told me that a widow shouldn't be splurging on renting a second room. I smiled when they told me I should save money for my daughter instead. I wasn't going to tell them the extra room was to ensure that daughter and sons didn't tangle their legs under the bed. I laughed and looked foolish, and let my neighbours walk around feeling smarter.

Sometimes you wish you didn't know things about your children. I knew my daughter would have loved to have the regular set of mother—father pushing her to get married from the time she was sixteen. Sadly for Radha, I told her early on that there was going to be no dowry and no huge wedding. But I'd somehow find money to pay for her to study whatever she wanted, I promised. Radha thought this was me being cunning. She knew that I knew that she didn't want to go to school at all. When she came home, she demanded I pay for a beauty parlour course. She was bristling from the top of her head all the way down her thin, flat chest like one of the roosters my grandmother used to keep. She must have thought I'd refuse. I agreed right away, and only asked to go to the parlour and speak to the woman about what she'd teach Radha for six months. Radha looked a bit deflated then, but she had chosen well. She goes to the parlour every morning with a bounce and a whistle that I've never seen in ten years of school-going. She's nineteen and truly enjoys having her own money to buy a cellphone. Or, recently, the home pedicure kit she's been unleashing on the neighbours. Perhaps her disappointment that I wasn't going to be like the parents of her jigri dost, Guddi from the next lane, would lessen with time.

This evening, I thought I heard a flirtatious note in Guddi's greeting to Vijay when he came home, but that was just me being my chudail self. She's always been fond of the boys since she has no brothers herself. They're not bad girls, Radha and Guddi.

Guddi's been married two years now. When she returns home from Faridabad once in six months, she comes in eye-watering orange and magenta regalia, determined that no one should forget she's a married woman now. As if I hadn't known her when she was a nine-year-old who gave my daughter headlice. As if I didn't know that this summer, when the water stopped coming in her parents' lane for fifteen days at a stretch, her father told her: 'Stay at your sasural, don't visit us in the summer anymore.' His pride couldn't bear her borrowing two mugs of water from the neighbours to wipe herself every morning.

I had my own reasons for wanting Guddi to leave. I was lying in bed a few days after the accident—hot, achy, uncomfortable—when I overheard her and Radha gloating over Guddi's husband's victory. He'd finally bullied his father-in-law into buying him a new motorcycle. 'Now I can hold my head up again,' said Guddi. 'I was sick with shame when I realised Papa thought he can get away with a scooter the way he had with both my didis. Who rides a scooter these days?'

I heard my daughter giggling loudly in agreement. Who rides a scooter? Nobody, I thought. Certainly not Guddi's presswala father, who's been cycling 3 km to his stand under the tree in Malviya Nagar for twenty-five years. I wanted to get out of bed and slap Radha and Guddi.

I've never hit my children and now was hardly the time to begin. And besides, the late evenings is when my body hurts the most and I was at my most irritable. I told myself I *had* to rest for my bones to knit together so that I could get back to work.

The school did not cut my salary for my first month in bed. And then school closed. But when school reopens, they might hire someone else. Never mind how much they say they love my cooking and how they put my picture in the annual magazine six out of the fifteen years I've worked there.

My aches were not much better this morning. The children were a little tired of their own limited cooking and were grumpy. I creaked out of bed, crouched over the single burner and made the pretty yellow dal with flecks of palak they secretly like almost as much as Maggi. Vijay insisted he was fine and dressed for school. Having managed to stay on my feet for a bit, I didn't want to go back to the sweaty bed. I walked about a little in the corridor.

Gulshan from the floor below was standing in his baniyan-chaddi drying his clothes on the railings of the metal stairs. I looked away, partly to avoid his gaze and partly to avoid looking at the staircase. In a few weeks, I'd have to go to the hospital again. The thought of getting up and down these stairs made me want to weep. When the ambulance first brought me back to Begumpur, I had to be carried up like a sack of rice. The boys couldn't manage, poor skinny things. Gulshan's older brother and Gurpreet, the landlord's nephew, and two other men I didn't recognise from the street groaned and huffed as they heaved me up the five flights. As I was turned around the third landing, I saw Manu biting his lip as he followed us. I caught his eye and in a flash of understanding I knew he was trying not to laugh at his elder brother. Poor Vijay was mortified to be dependent on other men to help his mother, and even more so because he wasn't sure if the men were copping a feel of his mother's fat ass. Manu's rolling eye was making me laugh, my broken hip stabbed me like a sword and I cried instead. I had forgotten about that moment till just now.

Behind me I heard Radha say bye and clatter down the stairs almost before I could leverage my whole body around to face her. I turned around again and went closer to the railing to see her walk down the street. There she went, already missed-calling on her cellphone, blithe as she pleased, tiny smug smile tugging her lips. The missed call operation baffles me and enrages me almost equally. Radha, for instance, never actually calls me when I'm at school. She only gives me missed calls and expects me to call back. 'No balance' is her perpetual excuse. Radha, Guddi and gang all have missed call codes for each other. So many rings for whatever message.

Then there're the boys who just ring random numbers and say hello-hello until they reach idiot girls like Guddi and Radha who coo back, 'No, *you* tell me your name first. No, why should I tell you who I am? Where did you get my number? No, my name is Guddi. There is no Sonali here. It's *Guddi*. I live in Begumpur. No, I'm quite fair. No, I'm not Sonali, I'm telling you. Hee hee. *You* shut up.' After a couple of times of listening to this radio drama, I thought the top of my head would come off like a faulty pressure cooker. I screamed at both of them that only fools would start romancing wrong numbers.

The hospital visit was more disastrous than I'd expected. I hadn't realised how scared I'd be crossing the road. I kept feeling the car hit me over and over again. Back home, on the stairs up, I stumbled and fell and banged up my knees. Vijay felt guilty for not preventing it, and so he'd been snapping at me. Manu skipped up to me and told me with unusual seriousness, 'Ma, you must lose weight. I saw on TV that if you become thin, you won't get heart attacks that easily.' Heart attack. I could hit that doctor for throwing that phrase about in front of the boys after checking my blood pressure. It is a bit high, my BP, but how can I cook without tasting for salt when I go back to work?

When Radha came in, I was feeling very sour. I've been telling myself recently that I must not become one of those women who've forgotten what it was like to be young and happy. But Radha's hints about marriage have been exploding and flying about the house like mustard seeds lately. First, there was the Three Days of Tragedy.

From what I pieced together through eavesdropping and police-procedure interrogation, her current love interest is a friend of Guddi's husband. He's in the cellphone-repair business in Nehru Place and has won the girls' hearts by regularly giving them movies they can watch on their phones. Now they no longer had to go to the guy who hung out on the Begumpur main road and pay him to transfer any new movies into their phones. All the neighbourhood parents suspected that he mostly stocked blue movies, so it wasn't that easy for the girls to go to him undetected.

Radha and this new guy—their thing's been going for a few months and, of course, he truly loves her. So much so that the first chance he got, he agreed to marry some girl his parents picked. For three days, Radha refused to go to work, crying, weeping, staring into space and, to my shock, she refused to even drink water. If I could've gotten out of bed, I would have prised her jaws apart and stuffed food down her throat. Manu, always the clever one, made fun of her the fourth day, saying, 'Didi, you're so thin, you look like a boy anyway. I don't know what'll happen. Who'll marry you now?' Radha threw a plastic bottle viciously at his head. Manu was hit quite hard but didn't hold a grudge. He laughed loudly and went to school. Radha ate something.

That evening, Manu came home from school with a furry, white rat in a box. Before I could exert my ritual sacrcasm about his zoo, he announced that his English teacher had asked his address so he could come and enquire after my health. Vijay growled, 'Of course, of the sixty kids in your class, your teacher wants to come and visit only your mother when she's stuck in bed. Tell him that we may not have a father, but our mother is not unprotected.' I held in my giggles. I looked at the floor and tried to look grave and grateful. Manu saw me smiling and Radha looked at me speculatively.

In a moment of weakness that night, when we were both ready to sleep, she told me that if only she had been the right caste, Manoj'd have married her for sure. For once, I held my tongue in the dark and didn't tell her how stupid she was. And who knows, maybe she was right. Maybe to some young men caste does matter as much as love. Raja and the boys I remember from my teens in Jharkhand, God bless them, they never discriminated. Any girl who was enthusiastic was good enough for them. Raja didn't even care I was Christian when he married me. 'I just want the right to squeeze your thighs when I feel like,' he'd whispered into my ear as we rattled about on the floor of the train to Bhopal.

Encouraged by what she thought was my forbearance, the next day after work, Radha told me that she had talked to *him* again. He'd consoled her that they could still be together even after he got married. This time I was speechless with rage. Radha mistook this for some sort of Guddi-like complicity. She thought I was her friend! She babbled on about how she'd spoken to him for two hours on the phone and had snuck out of the parlour early feigning illness to meet him. Soon everything would be alright, Manoj had promised. I rolled over in bed and faced the wall. Radha didn't notice at first.

After a while, she put her stick arms around me the way she used to as a child and tried to hug me. The girl was so pathetically skinny. What kind of mother was I that I couldn't feed my daughter and make her look like a woman? Perhaps I could cut parts of my excess flesh and give it to her. The insides of my head went dark with anger and I got up. I shoved her hard. Radha fell down. I looked down from the bed at her shocked little face. 'I don't want to hear anything more about this Manoj,' I told her. 'He sounds like a useless loafer. What does he mean by saying you can still be together when he's planning to marry someone else in a few months?'

She screamed at me then. What a terrible mother I was. How I'd sent her father away to die. How if she had a father she would have been married with a home of her own. How I preferred the boys to her. She had to work for a living so that the boys could go to school. I screamed back that she'd certainly never given the boys a rupee from her earnings. She yelled that she'd always known I was jealous of her. I had been cooking for years and I only earned a little more than she earned at the parlour. On and on until the landlord's wife came up looking extremely upset. I hated having to see her when I was sweaty, unwashed and close to tears. Next year, when her middle son got married and brought home a bride, for sure she would use this fight as a reason to evict us.

I wronged her there. Gurmeet knocked Radha lightly upside the head and told her to go breathe some fresh air on the roof. And pluck some pudina leaves from the pot while you're there, she said. Radha went up, heaving and sobbing. Gurmeet didn't say much, asked me if I was feeling better, muttered something about unmarried girls and left.

Radha didn't talk to me for a week. Not even when the neighbours came running to say there was a snake in the building and they wanted Manu to catch it. I pretended the fight hadn't happened and went about as usual. I didn't attempt to win her over either. She refused to sleep in the same room as me. She bullied Manu into sleeping on the floor next to me and went to sleep in his place before Vijay could object. Vijay was moderately respectful of his sister, but he was a greater stickler for propriety than even me. He didn't like her being rude to me. Then he got into a fight with her because she was on the phone half the night. He told me huffily that she'd been on the phone with 'woh', demanding his fiancée's number. Clearly, 'woh' had thought this was a very bad idea and had refused. Back and forth the missed calls went. And the tears and the hissing fights and Radha's attempts to somehow finagle the number out of him. Vijay said, 'I don't understand what Didi is up to. She kept telling him that she wants the number *just like that*. That she wouldn't call the other girl. That doesn't make any sense at all.'

The upshot of this was that Manu and Vijay ganged up and refused to share a room with her. She was back, stuck under my nose. By then, though, I was just fed up with her brainless behaviour. I wished I was better and could go to work and get away from the children. On the other hand, perhaps the accident had happened so that I could be at home and see what my children are up to. I dismissed the sentimentality instantly.

Radha unbent and began talking to me again. We had a bit of a stumble one evening, but that too didn't last long. She had come in beaming and said, 'Ma, look at my face.' I was trying to clean the room without breaking my hip again. 'What is it?' I asked. 'Guess, guess,' she said. 'Look closely. Don't you see any difference?' I regret it now, but I snapped, 'I don't care what you've done to your face. I'm not interested in this beauty rubbish. I just like to see healthy, happy faces.' Radha was instantly miffed and who can blame her?

But the next morning, she woke up in a great mood. I was standing near the stairs as I watched her go. All the way from the fifth floor, from the end of the lane I could hear her brain humming like a hill of red ants. My stomach clenched and unclenched at the thought that I'd begun to dislike my daughter.

How ashamed my mother would be of me. She had such pride in us girls. As much pride in me as she had in my older sister, even though some birth defect kept Didi like a ten-year-old all her life. But my mother always praised her for helping run the house: helping our grandmother with the cooking, cleaning, fetching things, washing clothes.

My father had had no doubt about how my mother would react when she heard the news on her return. She had been away a week in Ranchi, accompanying the staff of the school she worked in. And a week was long enough for one of my half-brothers to settle like a fat snake in our house. Papa was fond of his sons from his first marriage, but mother's steady gaze usually kept them at a distance. In the middle of that week, when I came home after school, I found my bastard half-brother squeezing and poking and twiddling Didi. She, poor thing, was alternately laughing and crying, and afterwards told me that he'd done this to her the previous day too. I was ten, so Didi must have been sixteen then. I told my grandmother, and she tore into the bastard and told him to leave the house. But he thought he had the measure of my grandma, so he stuck around smirking at us women. My father, on the other hand, had no doubt about what his wife would do when she returned. He didn't shout at his son or slap him as I thought he would. Instead, he pulled some money out of the pockets of a fraying pair of trousers hidden in the back of a cupboard, went to the backyard and found my half-brother. He thrust the money at him and told him to leave town immediately. 'Catch a train to Patna,' I clearly heard him say when I followed him to the backyard, hoping to see my half-brother bleed from his nose.

That night, I told my grandma I would no longer make rotis for my father, and she only said, 'Alright.' The next morning, my father asked for a glass of water and

I ignored him. The truth is, I've never spoken to him since. My mother, back from Ranchi after the school trip, heard the news from us. She was so terrifying in her rage that none of us dared speak to her. After a few months, she calmed down and resumed her normal, clipped exchanges with Papa. Several times, Didi accused me in her piping voice of being mean to our father. Papa could not hide his winces whenever she'd say this. He tried over the years to bully me into forgiving him, but I never did. I didn't go to his funeral even. My mother never asked me to.

The only time my mother was truly ashamed of me was when I first tried to run away with Raja. It gave my father, my uncle and one of my half-brothers permission to beat me up, permission to tie Raja in a sack, ready to drown him in the river. I had to sneak out of my house and get to the sack before they did. Raja and I left home again that night. Six months later, we were in Delhi. Six years later, I had two children and a cleaning job in Ritu Madam's school lab. Seven years later, I had three children, a cleaning job in the school canteen and the satisfaction of kicking out a cheating husband. I didn't go to his funeral either, and I'd be hard-pressed to tell you what he died of.

Lying in bed with nothing to do was making me maudlin. I spent too much time thinking of the past.

I was at that odd stage of recovery when I was too unwell to do much but too healthy to be patient anymore. It's the kind of mood in winter I'd assuage by busting my budget on red carrots. The slow, patient making of gajar halwa made me feel better on the days it was too cold to do much else. But summer in Delhi with three broken bones and a cast? I wouldn't wish this itch on my worst enemy.

Vijay must have sensed my restlessness when he came home. Perhaps because they had no father, perhaps because we'd been living in each other's armpits, or perhaps because I had had them so young, my children have always been sensitive to my moods. Vijay asked me to help him draw diagrams in his science lab book. I taught all three kids to draw, but lately I've needed to do very little of it. I taught them to read English too by getting Ritu Madam to teach me first. After I finished one diagram, I was exhausted. Squinting and holding the pencil steady had wiped me out. I fell asleep without eating dinner. I woke up at some point and found all three kids crouched like little owls in the dark, watching TV at the lowest volume possible. The fish were still in their shoals, but the baby shark swam restlessly and gleamed at me.

All of the next day I was tired and restless. I cleaned both rooms slowly: dusting, folding, wiping, sweeping. I spent the whole day doing it. It was by accident that I found my savings certificates in Radha's trunk, carefully folded between her two best chunnis. It was the Rs 20,000 savings certificate Ritu Madam had put in my name before she left for Pune. I dug around more and also found my passbook in there. I tasted a backwash of one of the pills I'd eaten that morning. I quickly looked at the last page and found no new entries. The Rs 50,000 I had saved pai-pai for the kids' education was still there.

I put the papers back in my trunk. When Manu returned from school I asked him to help me move the TV; I hid the papers underneath it. He was puzzled but didn't ask why his mother was looking crazed.

When Radha came home, we had a doozy of a fight. She showed no guilt, no remorse. She had only questions. Why hadn't I told them I had all this money ferreted away? Why had I lied that there was no money for a dowry or a wedding? What was I planning to do with the money? Unfortunately, it became a three-way fight, because Vijay walked in unusually early from the gym. He was nursing a sore thumb from a weight he'd dropped on it. I've rarely seen him so angry. 'You keep quiet, Didi. Ma doesn't need to explain herself to you. She doesn't need to give her money to you so you can give it to that useless Manoj. That's what this is about, isn't it? I know. I called and spoke to Guddi Didi's Ranjeet Bhaiya, and he told me Manoj's family has already spent the dowry on fixing up their house, so he'll *have* to marry that girl. And if you find some money and give it to him, then of course he'll happily marry you. Why would you marry him? He doesn't even have a proper job. That cellphone-repair shop threw him out last month.'

Radha screamed and tried to claw Vijay. I jumped out of bed, but only managed to knock Manu over and wind him. He scrambled up and stood protectively in front of the fish tank. I almost laughed. Vijay was holding Radha's hands together in one of his giant hands. 'Don't hurt your sister,' I said sharply. But Radha was beyond protecting. She spat and wriggled and raged, the lines of sequins on her salwar suit making me feel slightly dizzy. Vijay let go and she tried to go at him again. 'What do you know about love, you giant black monkey? Who could love you? God knows who your father is. God knows who she slept with and produced you.'

It would've been better if she'd just clawed Vijay's eyes out. The poor boy was so sensitive about being dark like me when his siblings were fair like their father. After years of telling him that everyone from my family was this colour, I'd even caved in and let him buy his creams. Not that they worked. I wanted to wring Radha's neck. The girl seemed possessed by a demon. Then I registered what she'd said, that I'd cheated on her father. I looked at Vijay and saw from the downturn of his mouth that he would always wonder if it was true. And just like that, in the flutter of an eyelash, the demon was inside me.

'Radha,' I said with such coldness and calm that she stopped shoving Vijay and turned to glare at me. 'What I do with my money is my business. Perhaps I might've given some of it to you some day. But you've clearly lost your mind. So you have two options. You can go back to living under my roof with my rules—as you once did. Or you can leave now.'

Radha's eyes grew as big as plates, like the faces in the cartoons Manu still liked to watch. She tugged her hands free and stomped off to the other room. The boys slept scrunched up like prawns on the floor of my room. The light stayed on and none of us had the energy to switch it off. From the next room, we heard fragments of conversations. At first there was passion and force in Radha's voice. As the night progressed, we heard only whines and moans. We didn't stir or speak.

Around dawn, I woke up to the sound of Radha's voice. She was still on the phone? 'What is the point of saying that you wished I was your daughter, Shefali Didi, if you won't help me? I need to leave this house. I can't breathe anymore. I can't eat. I can't sleep. I have to leave. No, I don't want to wait till morning when I come to the parlour. I have to leave now. No, no, I'm not coming to the parlour. No. Bye.'

I felt like the car that hit me was now parked across my chest. Should I cry? Will crying show her that her mother loved her? I couldn't remember the last time I cried. If you didn't count weeping from pain after the accident.

I could hear her charging about in the next room. Manu woke up at some point. He fed the fish, pulled the single burner out and made Maggi for all of us with his usual dispassionate efficiency.

It never feels like these times will ever end, but fortunately they do. We were all tightly sprung like coils the first few days. Radha came and went without explanation. The boys skirted around her. More days passed. We had our first conversation. She began sleeping in my room with me again. I had another hospital visit. I could go back to work in a week, the doctor said. I prayed the drama would end before my long work days began.

School reopened and I only missed a few days of work before I rejoined. It felt good to be standing square before my stove again. I got them to put a chair in the kitchen so I could cut vegetables and knead atta sitting down. Class IV made me a huge get-well-soon card for craft class. Radha made fun of it, saying that only Manu's art was worse than theirs.

Was Manoj back in her life or not? I wasn't sure and I didn't want to ask. I saw her watching movies on her phone and guessed that perhaps he was. But the missed call drama was playing less, so perhaps he wasn't. I even briefly wished Guddi was around, so I could grill her. I made a note to myself to go visit Guddi's mother. Sanctimonious cow though she was, she at least knew what her daughter was up to.

After a week at work I'd almost forgotten about my accident. Vijay's crushed thumb, though, just wasn't healing. I had to kick his reluctant self all the way to the doctor. He came back looking terrified. The doctor had told him that in a few days the thumb would've been so infected he'd have had to cut it off. I was a bit sceptical but I didn't contest it, given that the results were a nice, clean bandage and no more ooze. Radha took over the cooking grudgingly though she still ate painfully little.

The next day I came home and cleaned furiously. I must have overdone it, because a few hours later, I collapsed into bed, entirely unable to move. I slept soundly and dreamlessly. I woke up when Radha came in with her jangle and her bangles. She said something about making rotis, and I grunted and went back to sleep.

I woke with a start, I don't know how much later, and went into the other room. Radha was crouched over the single burner holding a phulka; it bloomed over the flame. I opened my mouth to ask about the rancid smell coming from the stove. She heard me enter and, startled, looked up with those big brown eyes that are so like mine. The fear on her face knotted my stomach and there was an ugly, metallic taste in my mouth. The demon in my head wanted to know, 'What's in the rotis? What is she doing?'

With a vicious anger I'd always known in me, I smiled at my frozen daughter. I swooped up the whole stack and flung it into the corridor dustbin. Radha straightened out of her crouch and trembled. And then she was gone. I heard her thin chappals clattering down the metal spiral. I went to the railing and saw her run down the street, her handbag and chunni leaping behind her.

I watched her and remembered my father handing my half-brother money for his getaway train. When my boys came home, I was going to somehow find the words to tell them what their sister had done.

Workout of the Day

W.O.D.

Chest-to-bar pull-up ladder

Rest 5 minutes

1/2 body-weight overhead squat ladder

For the ladder pattern, perform one rep the first minute, two reps the second minute, three reps the third minute, continuing as long as you are able. Use as many sets each minute as needed.

After his workout, Sanjeev spent a good part of Saturday morning on Twitter cursing the judge, flirting with contempt of court. Through breakfast he was at it, tweeting with his right hand and spooning up upma with his left.

In the car, as he passed Marble Market, he was briefly distracted. He marvelled, for the hundredth time, at how ridiculously beautiful the service road looked with the glittery glass quilt created by drunken boys and men who drank in their cars all of Friday night outside the liquor store and then threw the bottles in magnificent arcs out of their windows. In half an hour, the cleaners would be out to sweep it all away. Till next Saturday morning. It was the only bit of whimsy he ever saw in this suburban Delhi wasteland of vaguely Soviet architecture he had moved to four years ago.

After Marble Market, Sanjeev needed his wits about him to negotiate the road to Mahipalpur in reasonable time. Still, at long traffic lights, he quickly got back on Twitter and followed the continuing arguments around the case. Sanjeev thought rapists should be hanged. Or chemically castrated. That's the only way the bastards would learn. This morning at breakfast he'd thought he was going to have a stroke. How could the judge let those guys go after what they had done to that girl? Fucking woman judge! A woman judge at that! She should be ashamed. He intended to say so in his Monday op-ed.

People talked such shit online. Men were so sleazy. Leela and he often said to each other these days that they were grateful they didn't have any children, particularly that they didn't have any daughters. Of course they were stuck with Kuttan for some time. And since Leela's sister was showing no signs of getting better, it might be a very long while. First her useless son, then the divorce and then cancer. That woman just couldn't catch a break.

Start the day cursing rape on Twitter and that's the way the rest of the day was going to go, he thought to himself. In the newsroom, the conversation had been stuck in a loop for one year since the Delhi gang-rape.

Reportage on rape, op-eds on rape, day in, day out. But what was the use if the system was still stuck in the dark ages. What the fuck was that judge thinking?

At Mahipalpur, the light refused to change. He amused himself, for the hundredth time, by thinking that it was appropriate that the road that led to Dwarka was called Ulan Bator road, given that it'd seemed like Outer Mongolia when he had first moved.

In a while his thumb hurt, so he stopped scrolling and put his phone down. He switched off the ignition and rolled the windows down. On the motorcycle next to him, a young fellow had propped up his chunky tablet against the engine and was typing furiously. Sanjeev watched him for a while and then reached out through the window to tap his shoulder. The young man looked down, startled, eyelashes trapped against his spectacles inside his helmet. Sanjeev smiled. The young man flipped up his visor and looked enquiring. Sanjeev asked, *'Itna kaam hai kya?* No time to waste?'

The young fellow laughed a little and said, '*Kya karein*, Uncle.'

Sanjeev felt the sting of the Uncle less and less these days. A few years ago, it would have ruined his morning. Especially if it was some good-looking girl. But he had shaved his head and begun to wake up earlier and earlier to work out — regardless of how late he'd been out. He ate clean and lifted heavy. He certainly didn't eat the crap the rest of the newsroom ate.

The young fellow and he chatted for a few minutes. Sanjeev cast his eye over the boy's soft, white face and the equally soft belly and felt sad about the future of spondylitis and kneecap replacements that awaited him. He flexed his abs and rolled his shoulders happily under his new slim-fit coat. He liked winter in Delhi, but in winter everyone could hide their thick waistlines. In the summer, when he walked into the newsroom, he knew other men eyed his arms and his belly with irritation.

The light changed. The boy's eyelashes fluttered nervously. They quickly said their goodbyes and they were off. By the time Sanjeev hit Dhaula Kuan, he was fed up with the rape. The Monday op-ed he had been composing in his head was unravelling.

And by the time he hit the office, he was *done* with rape. Altogether. What was the point in writing about it when those animals were roaming the roads?

The office was shrouded in its usual twilight gloom at mid-morning. At his desk, he flipped through the papers, switched on the TV and put it on mute. He saw on Twitter that his former colleague Daljit Singh, fifteen years younger and not a hair on his head, had a book on India and China coming out. The cover was hideous and the title was instantly dragon-elephant-forgettable. In the way the book was going to be too.

He made a note in his to-do list to put the fear of God in every one of his reporters this week, especially Feroze. Elections were four months away and they were still doing all their itty-bitty, inconsequential nonsense stories. God, that whiny Feroze. Always a riot, always a stone-pelting that would not let him leave his house to do any reporting. What was the point of having a reporter in Kashmir?

Sanjeev pulled his list up and began thinking of which one of his lazy fucks to bumboo first. Then one of his UP contacts called. Thakur proceeded to tell him one hilarious, morbid, hopeless story after another. When the call was done, the near-empty, draughty office filled him with more irritation than before. What he wanted to be doing was hanging out in Lucknow with Thakur eating a big, airy bowl of makhan malai.

If Amit hadn't wanted to discuss their pre-election planning, he wouldn't have had to drive all the way in on a Saturday morning. He could have had a superb mid-morning run in the mild sunshine and made some rousing phone calls. Instead, here he was, waiting for the morning meeting, looking at the top of Associate Editor Bhavana Shankar's punctual head. He flipped some channels and looked at his long list of missed calls.

By 11.30 a.m., Bhavana had dutifully got to the small conference room ahead of him. She was her usual unsmiling self. Sanjeev couldn't understand why she was always so stingy-lipped. Bhavana was the only woman he knew who looked bad in a sari. Four years ago, when she first joined the paper, he had tried speaking to her in Malayalam and she had looked blankly at him. At some point, she told him tersely that she had grown up in Orissa and barely understood any Malayalam. Sanjeev had thought to himself that explained why she looked so small and emaciated, no breasts or hips. Imagine growing up in Orissa, he thought to himself, thanking his stars that his father's engineering degree had kept them firmly in Bombay.

At some point, of course, Bhavana-ji had stopped wearing her saris. She went on a junket to Hong Kong and came back to work with a new wardrobe of tiny purple T-shirts and tiny child-sized jeans. He overheard her saying to one of the young graphic designers—with whom Sanjeev observed she was unexpectedly chummy, given her tight-assness otherwise—that it was the first time in her life she'd felt like shopping because everything in the stores were her size. Hong Kong or not, kiddie-jeans or not, Bhavana-ji continued her Silent Night treatment of him and most of her fellow senior editors. What do you think is her problem, he had asked Amit, the Chief Editor, one day. 'Whatever, yaar, Sanjeev. She keeps her mouth shut and does her work. And there are no bloody duplicate headlines or big fucking bloopers on the pages since she came. Don't screw with her. Though from what I understand, your complaint is unrelated to any desire for screwing of any sort.'

Sanjeev had laughed but also quickly zipped his mouth. His dear boss and old pal Amit was a superb gossip, like all good editors. If Amit imagined he sniffed even a meagre sexual interest, there'd be no end to the stories he'd be telling.

Today, Bhavana was in a sari after a long while, and he was irritated again by her mosquito-bite breasts and matchstick arms. Why didn't she eat properly and work out a bit? He was on the verge of suggesting CrossFit to her when the rest of the lot came in and swiftly the morning meeting returned to rape. He felt a renewed interest in his op-ed. He said, 'I think we should take a provocative position.'

'Please yaar, Sanjeev, yeh I-want-to-take-a-provocative-position is like I-am-going-to-make-a-viral-video,' objected the fat Features Editor. 'You can make a video and hope it goes viral. You can write a piece and hope it provokes someone. What is this I-want-to-take-a-provocative-position?' Before Sanjeev could respond, people began laughing quietly. Amit laughed, not so quietly. Overriding the laughter and over-riding Sanjeev's response, Amulya continued, 'I mean the bloody judge can say that she's taken a provocative position. Now.' Everyone laughed again. Sanjeev judged the room rapidly and decided to laugh along. He made mental notes to hump Amulya and her vaulting ambitions soon.

Amulya was forty-something, wore tight white pants and red underwear and bent over a lot, flashing her underwear. She didn't smoke or eat meat but had the air of the greatest tamasik in south Delhi, so louche were her eyes, so knowing were her thick lips. She owned an apartment in Vasant Kunj (god knows how) and had got her Ford EcoSport two months before Sanjeev had, and in the lightning blue he'd had his eye on.

Sanjeev felt—no, he knew—she was gunning for his job. Lately, she had taken to spending less time organising the visits of Bollywood's greatest to the Delhi office for web-chats, and more time slouching around Amit's office discussing Kashmir and the Naxal problem and talking about doing some 'on-ground reportage'. Like she could go beyond south and central Delhi and not fall apart. Like she knew what it took to be News Editor. She could barely work up the energy to get on a plane and go to Bombay to interview Shah Rukh. So far, Amit had not fallen for her item numbers, but who knew how long that would last. And if he did fall for it, Sanjeev would be stuck with the Creature-from-Features all through election season. And that would be hell on earth.

Sanjeev shelved his op-ed plan. His plan was to say that rape victims should forget the useless legal system and just get financial compensation from the State. Why bother going through double trauma and the two-finger test and the court and all the media circus? The two-finger test. Just the thought of it made him shudder. But having the Creature-from-Features interfering with his election plan would be worse than getting the two-finger test, he thought. He smirked to himself. His phone was jiggling and vibrating every few minutes. There was real work he could be doing. Instead, they were dancing around Rape Central. Oh, now Amit was getting into it.

'Fucking Delhi is just so unsafe. What is it, the stats? A woman getting raped every five minutes? My niece was thinking of doing her PhD here and I told my brother, forget it. Just send her abroad. I can't take responsibility for keeping her safe through five or six years here.'

Sanjeev looked at Amulya and noticed that her face was mirroring Amit's rueful expression though her eyes remained their dirty, unimpressed selves. Clever girl. Sanjeev wondered whether she had also gone through some body language training the way he had as a kid in Toastmasters Club. *Quickly, Sanjeeva, get with the programme. She is up to something. What is it?*

Whatever she was up to, it didn't become too clear in this meeting. Though Amit did end up saying to her that maybe she should start a new series on women negotiating nightlife in Delhi. He said, 'Are they scared? Have they stopped going to parties? Have bar owners noticed fewer women on ladies' nights? Or are they getting out there but just buying more pepper spray? Maybe we should do a story called the Rape Economy. What do you think?' Amit laughed as he was making the suggestion but it was embroidered with a very slight uncertainty around the edges. An uncertainty he'd never have had one year ago, Sanjeev thought to himself viciously. And sure enough, Amulya laughed. She didn't behave as if Amit had been suggesting a serious story idea. Which he had been.

What the fuck! Amit hadn't been uncertain about his ideas even when he was twenty-five, when their aukat—his, Sanjeev's and other junior reporters'—was to wait, dogs under the tables, hoping for the morsels dropped accidentally by their seniors in the newsroom. And now, because Amulya had a uterus, she was an expert on what a good story was?

Before he had even realised it, Sanjeev asked Bhavana: what do *you* think? All six people in the room turned to her. All looking as surprised as he felt. Only Bhavana looked completely composed. She had more grey hair than he remembered. Didn't she have a small child? A boy? She said in the voice that always surprised him because of how deep it was, 'Lots of women in Delhi travel at night. Because they have work. I don't think it's an option for women working in parlours and shops to stay at home or say we will take only radio cabs.'

And there it was, the fucking cold shower that was Bhavana Shankar. Everyone in the room wriggled a little for a few seconds and then started speaking rapidly to get over the moment. The meeting finished a little earlier than it usually did.

He needed a whole new op-ed idea, since as a man, apparently, he was not allowed to have an opinion on rape. He had briefly mentioned two possibilities to Amit, and with his usual discipline, typed one out quickly on the Indian death row prisoner in Pakistan that everyone was weeping crocodile tears over. As if everyone didn't know he was a spy. After the first draft, he went to the coffee machine and was on his way back when he bumped into Bhavana again. Not quite bumped, but there she was in the long corridor.

'That was a good point you raised there, Bhavana-ji,' he said to her. She looked at him unhelpfully.

'Talking about women who have to work. We end up forgetting that in a place like this.'

'A place like what?' she asked.

Sanjeev said, 'Well, you know. A place like this, the women don't need to work. I mean some of these birds, the interns, they drive to work in better cars than I'll ever have.'

'That just means that only people who can afford to be free labour can afford to be interns here. If we paid interns, we may have a different class of people. And I don't know if all the women who work here *don't have to* work. That's not what I was saying. Also we have male interns from similar class backgrounds.'

'No wonder you are such a great desk hand. You never get the facts wrong. You never get the quotes wrong,' said Sanjeev. And you will always be a desk hand, he thought to himself.

Amit appeared at his side suddenly and hustled him off to his office. They gossiped about election coverage and discussed a new reporter they wanted to hire in Assam. Then Amit said, 'Oh-ho bhai! I'd completely forgotten that Bhavana has that total activist background. Until she said that thing about women needing to work. *Baap re baap*, I am really scared to open my mouth these days.'

Sanjeev said, 'It's all become quicksand. Things were so much simpler before.'

Amit said, 'What shit. When were they simpler?'

'Not *things*-things. Just speaking was simpler. Language was simpler. See, in Malayalam and in Hindi, the phrase for a female servant is "woman with a job".

Kaam-wali. Vela-karatti. That's what it is. That's the correct usage. A woman with a job is a servant.'

Amit guffawed. 'Listen, my dear Panini, you can please keep these etymological insights to yourself. Though, on most Mondays, boss, if anybody was willing to pay for my lifestyle, I'd happily stay at home. What is wrong with women? Why don't they exercise the choices they have? Your wife at least is smart. Look at mine, she is insane. God knows what she is doing. I don't even want to know what her new business is all about. Should I be worried that she is in Bangkok every month?'

Amit was about to slip into his usual humble-brag about his super-rich, serial entrepreneur Type-A wife, Sanjeev knew, so he made his exit.

After a quick Twitter break and an even quicker Instagram break, he went over the draft, did a few nips and tucks and filed the op-ed. Literally nothing was happening in the world on TV.

He was in the middle of his meeting with the Delhi reporters when the Patna correspondent called saying he *had* filed his story, but it had somehow disappeared in the system. And now he couldn't leave his house because the city had flooded. Sanjeev immediately put him on speaker phone and demanded to know the details of this natural disaster that had only affected his house, because there was no news that Patna was flooded. Or had he forgotten to file that? Oh, it was only his street, was it? Sanjeev reamed him out, gave him a new assignment and promised him that if he called on Monday saying he couldn't file then he, Sanjeev, would come to Patna to see him swim in the Ganga. His Delhi boys were laughing as they listened to Sanjeev's end of the conversation. They knew better than to try these stunts with him.

His new man in Bombay called. Sanjeev was in the middle of a fairly bullshit-free conversation with him when he saw an email from his wife. Instructing him about what to do with Kuttan over the weekend. As if she had not repeated everything three times before flying out.

This morning he had made sure, even though he was incensed by the Delhi High Court, to look into Kuttan's room before leaving for work. Twelve years old and snoring like a buffalo. Sanjeev couldn't understand why Kuttan wouldn't get up in the morning to run or work out. They had a world-class gym half a kilometre away and a decent one in the building. Instead, he drooped all day, slept all night and barely managed to get to the school bus on time.

Leela didn't let him push Kuttan out of bed at 5 a.m. the way he used to when the boy had first come to stay a year ago. Then, one time, she had gone to Kerala for a week to fall at her mother's sacred feet and everything had gone to pot. He had made Kuttan go running with him every morning. It didn't matter how much Sanjeev screamed at the idiot, he just wouldn't run fast. Then, that last morning, he started crying and wheezing and doing his convenient asthma thing, and Leela of course had to turn up from the airport just then. She didn't say a word. She just dropped her bags and hugged Kuttan and rubbed his back continuously. He didn't stop crying, needless to say. His cheeks quivered more and his face turned red.

Sanjeev had felt helpless. He asked Kuttan, 'You run a little bit like this and you are ready to die. What kind of a man are you?'

Kuttan suddenly didn't have any wheezing. He broke out of Leela's clutches and screamed at Sanjeev, 'YOU are not a man. YOU are not a man.'

Sanjeev had wanted to punch him a little to just stop the cheeks from quivering. He might have hit him too, but the idiot might have died. Died before his dying mother died. Stupid, pink-faced idiot, Sanjeev thought. What did it mean that, every year, Kuttan looked more and more, not like his mother or his aunt, but his uncle-by-marriage's ex-girlfriend. Parvati who had ripped him a new one for not paying attention to her and married some French guy. What a girl she had been. And when rage made her cheeks pink, he could never look away. He was too terrified to add her on Facebook even now.

Someone had been joking the other day at the Press Club that Sonakshi Sinha looked not like her mother Poonam and certainly not (thank god) her father Shatrughan. Instead, she looked like Reena Roy, Shatrughan's old girlfriend. Useless time-wasting specimens, Sanjeev had thought as he looked it up on his phone. Of course, someone had uploaded photos of Reena Roy and Sonakshi Sinha next to each other in one of those Celebs Separated at Birth lists. Stunning resemblance. The world was a strange place.

Sanjeev missed Pachu Uncle with a huge pang. Pachu Uncle would have got a big kick out of BuzzFeed. He would have enjoyed the Internet generally. Sanjeev thought often that he owed Pachu Uncle everything, everything, everything. If he hadn't pushed Sanjeev into Toastmasters Club when he was a flabby, shy, sixteen-year-old, everything would have been different. He had learnt to speak in public. Learnt to 'cut a joke', as Uncle used to say. Had the 'Ahs' and 'Ums' counted brutally out of him. Pachu Uncle had told him to get his body in order. Made him join a gym. Sanjeev was addicted to weights back then. It was only after he'd moved to Delhi that he'd gotten into running. Poor Pachu Uncle had dropped dead on the beach in the middle of a morning run. Sanjeev could never pass Juhu beach without feeling miserable. After Pachu Uncle died, he never felt the Bombay-versus-Delhi thing again, though in party conversations he picked his side depending on his mood. Uncle had been right. For a political reporter, there was nothing to do in Bombay. And he certainly had not missed his father's continuing panic about his only son writing about politicians. As a government servant, he could never get past the feeling Sanjeev was going to get into trouble by talking politics outside the house.

At 6.30 p.m., he decided to go get a drink with a politician pal. Though the man was wonderfully hospitable, Sanjeev felt tired afterwards. Smiling and listening was coming harder and harder to him these days. When he passed Lutyens Delhi, every house seemed like a place he had smiled and listened and grovelled his way into. There was the house of the prosperous politician who had taken one look at Sanjeev's twenty-five-year-old moustachioed self and seen a knock-kneed, clumsy boy. 'Please don't break anything,' the man had said before seating him next to priceless temple sculptures. Or the Haryanvi minister who had complained that Sanjeev's coke-addicted predecessor on the beat had borrowed 500 rupees from him. Or the celebrity lawyer with the dazzling female assistants who had joked to Sanjeev, 'They are also part of my ill-gotten gains.' Sanjeev had been even more dazzled by his relaxed turn of phrase than by the assistants. Twenty years ago, he had fallen passionately in love with Delhi while wandering in one of these lanes looking for some or the other famous person's house. The love seemed to be waning a bit.

At some point he realised he had left his phone charger in the office. It was 11 p.m. but he drove back. He wished with irritation that he didn't have to do all this extra driving around the week his driver was away. When he was rooting about in his cabin, Manish, one of the nice young fellows who had joined the desk, came over to say hello.

Manish admired his new coat and Sanjeev told him how one of his editors had taught him this—no cop in Delhi would stop your car if they saw a driver in the front seat and a man in a coat in a backseat. They had a quick smoke and Sanjeev teased him about his ongoing two-girlfriend problem. Manish said, 'Please, sir, I have heard about some things you have been up to in this building.' Sanjeev threatened violence and laughed. Then Manish told him, 'But you missed the best two-girlfriend problem this evening.'

They were standing on the stairs—the last bastion of the smokers in the office—when Manish narrated the truly sensational story of his comrade on the city desk who had been fired that evening by Bhavana Shankar. Rohit had been fired after six months on the job for being stoned/drunk/comatose all the time. The only person he ever spoke to in the office was his roommate Parthiv who was on the sports desk. Rohit and Parthiv had been fired together for being useless together. But too stoned to react, Rohit and Parthiv had sat staring at Bhavana for over ten minutes. Then—according to all-hearing, all-seeing Manish, who couldn't have possibly been there—Rohit had leant over the desk and said to Bhavana, 'You need to relax, Bhav.' At which point, Bhavana called a burly guy from admin for help to have them thrown out. Sanjeev did feel a little sad about having missed seeing Bhavana in a human avatar. But not for long, because Manish had more goss. Manish had found out on the grapevine that the reason Rohit was asleep at work was because he spent many nights stalking an ex-girlfriend, hanging out outside her house, knocking on her door, waking her parents.

Sanjeev said, 'What shit!'

Manish giggled a bit and said, 'No, sir, this much all of us have known for a few months. That's not the news.'

'What do you mean this is not the news? What is it then?'

'Well,' said Manish giggling harder, 'apparently that was only one of the extra-curricular activities that cost him his sleep. He was also busy bonking Parthiv.'

'Bonking who?' Sanjeev wasn't sure he had heard right.

'Parthiv, his roommate, sir,' said Manish, cheered by the sensation he had created.

'He was bonking that guy? WHAT? That's disgusting. Man, am I glad I don't hang out in this den of vice. I don't know why I come into this office.' And with that Sanjeev left, smiling and shaking his head.

A little past midnight he was driving back on the empty streets. Near Teen Murti, there was just a bouncing, noisy black Audi and a little red Santro ahead of him. Even through the mild fog, the figure in the Santro looked familiar. It was skinny-minnie, terminator of homosexual copy-editors, Bhavana Shankar. He drove a little faster to see if he was right.

He was, there it was, her judgemental head of curly hair. He waved at her, but the Santro took off with a sudden spurt of speed. Was she driving away because she had seen him?

Then it hit him that Bhavana thought it was some strange creep following her on the road. The realisation came in this order. First the grin that split his face. Then the sluggish awareness that something funny was afoot.

Then the realisation that Bhavana Shankar thought he was an eve-teaser/rapist. How surreal was this. Cow.

He accelerated and in a few seconds was in a good old-fashioned chase in central Delhi. The red Santro was fleeing. He could see Bhavana's little head, barely visible over the seat. Did she sit on a cushion?

Sanjeev wasn't tired or sluggish anymore. He was calm and refreshed. His body was as relaxed as it was after forty minutes on the rowing machine. He just stayed far enough from Bhavana's car that she wouldn't see his face in her rear view, just close enough to make her shit bricks.

Later, in bed that night, he thought to himself that the whole thing must have lasted just a minute or two, but right then it felt like a whole leisurely hour of chasing his red prey down the broad, empty roads. And when finally he was almost bumper to bumper, she panicked. She jumped a light, almost into oncoming traffic. Sanjeev laughed so hard, he had to stop his car to calm down.

He had driven home humming and went to sleep giggling.

Sunday W.O.D.
3 rounds for time of:
Row 50 calories
150 double-unders
50 walking lunges

Monday W.O.D.
In front of a clock set for 12 minutes with a 135-lb barbell:
1 minute of squat cleans
1 minute of push jerks
2 minutes of squat cleans
2 minutes of push jerks
3 minutes of squat cleans
3 minutes of push jerks

His Sunday had been filled with reports of a new rape, this time in a cab. He had pushed his boys to reach the victim for a first-person account. They had been useless, of course.

His Monday morning began with more arguments on Twitter. The arguments took him all the way from Dwarka to Connaught Place in the afternoon. After lunch, as his driver parked his car beside a red Santro, he remembered the Saturday night chase. Somehow he had forgotten about it for most of Sunday. And as he took the elevator, his body relaxed into that calm, meditative, rowing-machine happiness again.

He didn't see Bhavana. Had she not come in? That would be hilarious, if he had scared her into a flu. Scared the pittam out of her, as Pachu Uncle used to say.

At his desk, between phone calls, he remembered Vailia, his college ex who'd taken a job in Delhi a few years after he'd moved there. She'd called after work and he'd taken her enthusiastically to his room in Civil Lines. Suddenly, in his room, she was all reluctant and shawl-covered. Every half an hour between smokes she'd look out of the foggy window and say, 'I think I should leave.' He had promised to escort her back to her friend's house in south Delhi safe and sound, but as the night progressed and the shawl stayed on, his irritation grew. At two in the morning, he got up abruptly, feeling like he'd had enough of her waffling. He'd walked with her in the thick, white fog to the auto stand. After a while, an auto came by with the driver wrapped like a mummy in several beige shawls and mufflers of his own. He himself, Sanjeev remembered, had been in a t-shirt and pyjamas, unbothered by the weather. What it is to be young.

Vailia got into the auto. She looked out at him as if to say, get in, get in, it's freezing. But from his face, she'd realised that he had no intention of escorting her across the city in the middle of the night. And then coming all the way back! Women and their hypocrisies. She hadn't said a word, though. Vailia was too proud. She just looked at him. Then she said 'Chalo bhaiya' to the auto driver, who had not missed the silent interplay. Sanjeev had watched the auto drive away with its nervous cargo and gone back to sleep.

The potential new hire in Assam had been flown in. Sanjeev liked him right away, the spring in his step, his leather jacket and the slightly wild-eyed look. After the jolly interview, he had an unexpectedly jittery phone conversation with everyone's favourite billionaire's new point man.

As he went back to waiting for Bhavana to appear, he noticed his chest was tight. It was locked tight like a bank safe and he had to make himself relax deliberately with deep breaths. He did some work in a desultory way, shared some links on Twitter.

When Sanjeev saw her coming down the long corridor, he almost leapt out of his cabin. Shouldn't rush a punchline with his eagerness, he told himself. He slowed to a saunter. Fat Amulya was rolling slowly up behind her, but for once he was not scared of her dead, louche eyes. He was almost jumping up and down inside his beautiful coat. A coat he'd have never been able to wear if he'd stayed in Bombay. Sticky, dead city. Dead, dead, dead. There was Bhavana. And there was her expressionless face.

When she was close, when she had almost passed him, he said, 'I thought you were a brave little feminist.' She continued to look at him with her face as thoroughly wiped of expression as if she hired a kaam-wali to do it every morning.

'I have never seen a feminist as panicked as you were the other night. Have you ever driven so fast before? Jumped a light too!'

Sanjeev saw Bhavana's face moving slowly from expression to expression, like those morphing faces in that old Michael Jackson video. Confusion. Shock. More shock. His own face was stretched in the biggest smile.

He was about to laugh out loud but saw her face twist into rage. Sanjeev paused. 'Why are you angry?' he asked.

Her mouth hissed silently. He saw rows of small, perfect teeth pointing at him and then she was gone. She was furious! For what?

For some months, his desktop had had a picture of Shobhana, not a still from her movies but one of her in a regular sari and in the Nataraj pose. The sari messily falling from her rampaging right thigh as high as her head, her pallu flying in the air, not like those neat Bharatanatyam costumes. He wasn't too sure where the photo was shot. It wasn't on stage. It looked like a living room. It was like a housewife had gone nuts. If anyone asked, he talked about how he was such a fan of Shobhana's, but that wasn't it, really. He just couldn't take his eyes off that photo, the feeling that, for once, it was an image that was real, that got it, cut through all the crap. He wished he could take Bhavana by her hand gently to his laptop and show her the photo. Maybe then she would understand what he had tried to do for her on Saturday night and why she needed to get a grip on her feelings.

'Oh come on! No need to be so angry! I was just showing you what can happen to women if they don't take precautions.' He called out to her rigid skinny back as she walked away. He was trying to stretch his face into triumph again when he saw Amulya right next to him.

'You are a piece of shit, Sanjeev,' she said.

He tried to say something but was stumped by these women's ridiculous behaviour. The iridescent green of her eyelids shone like a reptile with ambitions as she rolled past him towards Amit's office. Her flesh jiggled inside her black leggings with sparkly white threads glittering like broken glass.

How Andrew Wylie Broke My Heart

The exact sequence of events is a little sketchy but I remember that day was the first time I was online all day. That's all I did because I had just got a high-speed connection at work *and* at home.

When had I become friends with who? Whom. Something. It was September I think. I was shitty depressed and then I went on artyhearts.com and then I slept with Manav in October.

No, I remember what happened first was this. Anita called, and since she was stuck with the twins, I felt obliged to visit. Actually, her sister-in-law had died of some terrible disease, and her brother had gone off the deep end and joined an ashram. Anita was secretly konjum Mother Teresa-type. Married only three months and she actually said she would look after the kids. Okay man, we said, but are you sure? She cried and said, 'I have to.' Okay man, we said.

Yeah, I think it was September, because the babies were about six months old and their mother had died when they were three months old. So, I went to see Anita and she was a total mess. Her house was a total mess. She had not combed her hair in days and she was desperate to go have a bath. I could see why she had called only me. Even on our most hungover days, no one from the gang would have ever seen her looking like that—no liner, no kajal. So soon after her strange bloody marriage, Anita would have not wanted to lose her babe status also. She had always competed with me, but now I only felt pity. Even her killer boobs and hair wouldn't help if she let herself go like this. She was really out of the market.

Of course, the babies were super well behaved when I was around. She came out of the shower smiling and cursing like an auto driver who thinks you lied about your destination. No one cursed like Anita. She was strong and smouldering. Like a female, Telugu-speaking cowboy. She could say babu with so much contempt, it would make men come. I used to think that men loved her because she always looked like she didn't remember their names. I mean, I can't count the number of times we have sat at a table in a bar and I had to make all the effort of being friendly to new people we've met because Anita couldn't be bothered. Somehow, Anita was not brought up to make uncle—aunty conversation the way I had. A major disability in Malleswaram, but somehow winning all contests in bars on Church Street. I could play hard to get too if I wanted, you know, but I think it is rude.

That day, we hung around playing with the babies and I was beginning to get bored when Anita's husband

Prakash came home. And he is a bit of a pain. See he doesn't talk too much. And then when he starts talking, you expect brilliant things because he has a brainy face. But he is a total bore and talks very, very carefully, like he is sealing an arms deal with the LTTE. So slowly that the words start separating and drilling your eardrums. And suddenly the sentence comes together and you realise he has said nothing special. Prakash drives me mad.

I spent a lot of time that month with Anita, and the more I saw of Prakash, the more amazed I was. He was a big bore but he also knew everything. For sure. He was the kind of guy who knew which model car cost how much in which city, where to stay in Udupi and where the office of the Registrar of Examinations was. He was a bit of a human Wikipedia and really well travelled, but he had so many theories about everything, and all said in that godawful, boring way. And he was a vegetarian and said he drank only single-malt whiskies.

One day, I asked Anita. I just couldn't help myself. 'Why did you marry Prakash?' Anita's face hardened. And I suddenly had a glimpse of that rum-and-coke drinking maniac who used to duck work, drag me out of college and introduce me to the strangest men. It's possible I might have stayed under my mother's thumb forever if I hadn't met Anita at yoga class. She used to amaze me because nothing frightened her. The very first time we were hanging out, she waved at a guy passing by. She smiled fondly and said to me, 'He likes my chest.' I was speechless. Another time we went clubbing somewhere and someone pinched her ass. She slapped him and went on dancing.

Now, when I asked her about Prakash, she didn't say anything. I didn't bring it up again. We went back to just hanging out, making filter coffee and gossiping as we usually did, babies or no babies. It didn't matter that it wasn't the shady bars we used to love going to when we had worked in the same agency.

One week later, I saw the ad for artyhearts when I was mind-numbingly bored. So, so bored that when I saw Venkatesh surfing porn I didn't march into Gonsalves's office to complain. I do that every once in a while when I see Venkatesh staring particularly stupidly at babudreams. com, a porn site for Telugu men. That expression of his irritates me so much that I launch myself into Gonsalves's office and pretend to be very scandalised at my colleague looking at obscene material during office hours.

But that day, I was so bored I looked over Venky's shoulder, saw a nice banner ad for artyhearts.com and opened it on my system without thinking. Then I was completely, totally charmed. It was the cutest thing. Artyhearts was supposed to be a dating site for intelligent people. Clean, white design, really funny content and interesting guys. I didn't know there were interesting guys in Bangalore. I mean it was 2006, but Bangalore was just dead. Even the *Times of India* could not make Bangalore parties look posh. But there were all these really cool-looking types on the site. More than one moron had uploaded Shah Rukh Khan's face as his profile picture. But never mind.

That month, I was trying to work on the brand image of a Haryana-based towel company. And I had the most idiotic ideas for it. I was spending days writing copy that no one was ever going to use and looking over the portfolios of the South African male models that we were flying in to look like upmarket towel-buying Indians and I was imagining screwing them. It's just horniness I know... but what to do. Towels! One thing that came out of all the time I spent on artyhearts was that I told the daft client he should consider a little research on upmarket singles with disposable incomes. He looked doubtful about unmarried people staying clean and then we went on as usual.

Meanwhile, I had got fully excited by artyhearts and posted my profile. Deleted it and rewrote it and uploaded some pix. I conned Sugunan, the agency photographer, into taking some pictures of me as if I was just checking out the possibilities of my new digicam, and Sugs being Sugs took 40 lakh pictures. I looked great. Fresh and fair. A little fat but my skin looked great. So, uploaded two of those and then one by candlelight I took of myself after lots of juggling.

I tried to figure out whether to ping some boys or wait to be pinged. Offline, I am a pinger. I don't like sitting round waiting. Online, I thought it might be fun to see what happens. Some fuckers from Macedonia and Munnar and Jhumritalayya were already sending me can-i-make-friendship-with-you-mails but I don't think they cared whether I was a goat or a cow as long as I had a girl's name. One guy sent me a picture of his dick. It's a thing online.

One boy called Syed messaged me and he seemed really sweet. We exchanged a few mails and he began by talking to me about beaches. We met for coffee, but it was a big mistake. He was average-looking and not tall. He kept asking me about my views on politics, a woman writer called Irshad Manji and about progressive Islam. I kept longing for the kind of evil Muslim in a Pathan suit they had in the old, trashy movies, who would at least look seductive and laugh a big laugh and stroke his moustache. Syed had a face like the kind of pavum foreigner who comes for a two-week holiday to Bombay and has diarrhoea throughout. Someone who would never manage to get to the great spots despite months of planning. The problem with Syed, apart from looking like someone who would always get cheated by Bangalore auto-drivers, was that he was so into current affairs. I have not read a newspaper in years and I don't really care. Except, I think that reservations are really stupid. If you ever lived in the real world, like I have, you'd see the kind of people who get away with hell because of reservations and you'd totally agree with me.

None of the other cool ones messaged me. There was one guy who was a sound engineer and he looked so amazing that I didn't know why he was on a dating site. He was sensationally tall and had beautiful eyes. But there he was. I simultaneously felt better and worse. If he can't find someone, then why should I worry? And if he can't get someone, what chance for me? I messaged him with my heart going dub-dub. He sent me a fairly rude-but-pretending-to-be polite mail saying that I didn't seem his type.

I think that was the week when I didn't do anything at work but hang out on artyhearts. I had almost got bored with artyhearts when I saw Manav online and decided to message him. Manav was some sort of techie and actually lived close to me. We quickly made arrangements to meet, but then he had to unexpectedly go to Chicago on work. So we messaged each other a lot and mailed and said deep-type things to each other. After two weeks, he was back and we met a few times for dinner. Manav had really long, curling eyelashes, but he was one of the worst kissers I have ever met. And he was a thin, brooding type. He said some terrible things to me. Particularly about the colour of my inner thighs. I really don't like people who affect my self-esteem and damage my body image. So that was the end of Manav.

I snapped out of my trance, went and hung out with my friends. They were all like, where have you been! What do you mean you were online? What do you mean you were dating online? But when I told them the details, all of them wanted to join artyhearts as well.

That week when I went to see Anita, she was thrilled to bits to see me. I told her some of the stuff I hadn't told the others. Like how when I saw the penis, I had not immediately screamed and run away. I found it funny and had continued conversation with the owner of the penis.

And the shit Manav had pulled in bed before telling me to see a dermatologist for my inner thighs. She laughed and laughed.

Then I realised Prakash was just outside, eavesdropping. I got damn bugged. I glared at him and fell silent. Prakash recommended some new books on Internet dating, including one on the history of artyhearts. Whatever. I left after some time. The thing is, I knew Prakash thought Anita and I were slutty girls. Anita was now reformed and married, but I was still clearly a slut. I didn't like the idea of his knowing about my adventures on artyhearts.

I didn't visit Anita and the babies for a week. She called. Said 'what's up?' I chattered about something or the other and then she hung up. After that, it was a bit like a late library book. Now that I hadn't visited Anita in a while, I couldn't go at all. Maybe this friendship was over, I thought. We were in different phases of our lives, I thought. Not that this phase of my life was getting me laid.

After the Manav fiasco, I was really depressed. I was beginning to almost feel I should stop sleeping around and get married. (Obviously not to a Prakash. Never sleep with a Manav. Never marry a Prakash.) I said something about it on my artyhearts status message. A girl called Poon messaged me saying dating sites made her feel that way too. She was a fashion photographer in Bangkok and we started chatting. It was great to get to know some other culture. I mean, we Indians really don't make an effort to understand other cultures. And we don't travel enough, I felt. That is why we are so narrow-minded.

Poon was really exciting. She was half-Thai, half-Burmese and really gorgeous. She had a lot of boyfriends, and in Thailand apparently it's okay to have many boyfriends. Here...you know! It was damn good to talk to her because she was not one of those annoying liberal Americans. Neither was she some good Iyer girl in a software company whose profile on artyhearts would be, if ever she was on artyhearts, 'I am shy but I have a good sense of humour.' Poon was constantly dating and her parents knew and all. It was superb and I envied her. I chatted for hours with her. I bitched about my men and she bitched about hers. We talked about work also. She made a lot of money but was expected to suck up to her clients. Which she never did. I was so thrilled to meet someone who was as rude as I was to clients. And her clients were loonier than mine. Poon had even worked in Bollywood, so she told me lots of insider gossip. I could not believe some of the stories! I mean, people say that advertising people sleep around, but Bollywood!

When I passed on some of the gossip, especially that of a father and son, both actors, sleeping with the same woman, my offline friends refused to believe me. My online friends were, I realised, much cooler. I was chatting with a Japanese man in Australia who was working in a bank, a Pakistani writer in New York, a Mexican model and a scientist in Bangalore. The Mexican model and I were surprised by how similar our mothers were. When his sister was getting married, he sent me an invitation. The Pakistani writer Cyrus from

NY was Parsi, not Muslim, and very sweet. He even burnt some fantastic music for me and sent me CDs. He said he got tired of typing Dakshayini and shortened my name to Dexter.

In December, Poon, my Thai friend, who I was beginning to think of as my best friend, took off for a holiday. I was feeling damn bad because she was going off for a month to some place without Internet. Poon's sister had a tragic life. After her husband died, she had joined a monastery. Once a year, Poon visited her in the monastery.

That month, I became closer to Cyrus, the Pakistani writer, and to Milly, who was an artist in Singapore. Poon had known Milly from her university days in the US. I really missed Poon when the writer-chap started hinting that he would like me to come to New York and be with him. Come on, Dexter, come on. I kept typing *rofl*, but it was such a cool idea. If Poon had been around I could have discussed it with her. I felt like I could tell Poon anything.

Unlike Poon, her artist friend Milly was not interested in men at all. One day, she asked me whether I had ever had any lesbian relationships in school. I was very angry with her but she was only joking. In any case, Milly was only interested in her work and travel. She told me that she had written a book on art and it was going to be published. It was her third book. I saw her first book on Amazon and I thought how awesome it was that I was friends with a Thai-American living in Singapore who had two books to her credit.

Actually, my older cousin is quite a famous writer. In Tamil but still…Everybody in Tamil Nadu knew her and she is only four years older than me. Her mother, my Periyamma, used to blame my parents for sending my brother and me to a school where we did not learn any Tamil. My mother would say, 'That's true. That's true,' but she would laugh scornfully after Periyamma left. 'As if I want my daughter to have that thick accent and be constantly smelling of beans poriyal.' My brother and I were not so sure. I thought it was cool that even some of our distant super-old aunts were fans of my cousin's writing. Even though she was really into Dalits and stuff.

I mentioned some of this stuff to Milly who asked me why I didn't write myself. I did, I mean I was a copywriter, but I had never really thought of fiction. Milly sent me a writing exercise and said, 'Try it. You might surprise yourself.' I fucking amazed myself. I wrote about my mother and our relationship and I cried throughout. When I mailed it to Milly, she loved it too. She wrote to me saying, 'Dearest Dakshayini, you are so talented and so young. Your piece made me cry.' Online, when we were chatting, she introduced me to an American writer-friend of hers. Again, a man from New York. Andrew was cute and funny. A bit old and he was really into some kinky stuff. A little too kinky even for me. Like he wanted me to be his slave and listen only to him. I made some joke about how he should get an Iyer wife from Tamil Nadu. But he didn't get it. He said some more things about collars and whips and I was like woah. I scream when the doctor tries to give me tetanus shots, so no way is some man spanking me or whipping me or whatever. Also, I had a college friend who used to say 'spank me, sponk me' instead of 'fuck me!', so whenever Andrew said something about spanking, I'd collapse laughing. So, after a couple of chat sessions, when he realised that I could only pretend to be an obedient schoolgirl for like five minutes before I got bored, Andrew gave up.

Once we had got past that slight embarrassment, we got to talking about writing. Milly had sweetly not mentioned to me that Andrew was actually a literary agent, one of the biggest in the world. I guess she had not wanted me to be nervous. I only found out when I googled him. There were hundreds and hundreds of articles about him online. I wondered how many people who knew him in real life knew that he was into such kinky shit—nipple-clips and ropes and stuff. He recommended some great books to read. After a few days, he asked me whether I wrote and I said that I had recently started writing fiction. He didn't sound too interested, but when he was signing off he said, 'Hey kid, do you write poetry? I am looking for hot young poets for a new project. I am doing some work with a well-known American musician.' Still not telling me he was this huge agent or any kind of agent. He was casual, so I played it cool too.

Here is the thing. I had looked up Andrew's client list and there was only one musician—Bob Dylan! I know I am a good person and I work hard and all that, but this really felt like someone up there in heaven was looking out for me. I thought about a girl I knew in college. She used to write really crap poetry. I mean, really crap. She posted stuff on a poetry forum online and there was an Indian guy from LA who read it and loved it and started writing to her. They became good friends and, a month later, he flew down in his private jet to propose. Anita and I used to be amazed that she had got a fibre-optics millionaire with her poetry. But now when Andrew asked me about my writing, so soon after I finally allowed myself to think I can write things other than copy for towel ads, it felt like freaky shit. I felt so humbled.

I agonised for a day or two about what to send Andrew. What would Bob Dylan like? I downloaded his entire discography as the pros call it and went to sleep with it playing on my headphones. In the middle of a client briefing, I was suddenly inspired. I needed to write my ideas down immediately, but I was sitting in the conference room with some senior exec from the towel company. I smiled sweetly at him and said, 'Hold on for a second.' I made him sit twiddling his thumbs for five whole minutes while I wrote what he thought were notes for the towel ad. I was of course writing a song for Bob Dylan. When I finished, I smiled at him again and we went back to the briefing.

That evening, I finished three songs and sent it to Andrew. I didn't tell anyone because I didn't want to jinx it. But he mailed back within a day: Where have you been all my life? Who are you, you wild, wild little girl? There is some sensational stuff here. It needs some work, but what doesn't? I'll talk to you soon.

I thought to myself—this is how people get discovered. One day you are just walking around like an aam aadmi and then you are on some other level altogether! At this point, I was finding it difficult to keep it to myself. So I wrote to Milly and Poon. Poon was still out at the monastery, so I didn't expect to hear back from her. Milly wrote to me promptly. 'So excited for you. Trust Andrew to know instinctively that you are a poet. Let me know how it goes, my lovely. Btw, I *was* reading and highly recommend *Scents of a Royal Rug*, a poem by a Thai poet called Sukothai. It's about a washerman who loves the scents of women from the palace whose clothes he washes. It's long, philosophical, erotic and great in Thai. Unfortunately it doesn't translate well as poetry. I was introduced to Sukothai by an older grad student engaged by my father to teach me an appreciation of the arts, I am glad we explored in full measure with Sukothai as a trusted guide. Ahh Jong!' I wondered how Poon and Milly had such exciting lives while I had to do this shit job every day in Bangalore where nothing ever fucking happens. Ahhhh Jong! Wait for Dylan-san.

When I saw Cyrus online a few days later, I just had to tell him. I was sure he would understand. He started guffawing! 'Bob Dylan! But he would never use someone else's lyrics. No way!' I was really cold to Cyrus and signed off. I should have guessed he'd be jealous. After all, he had been shuffling around New York for *years* pretending to be a writer. He was already thirty-one without being published.

Two weeks passed and I hadn't heard back from Andrew. I didn't see him online on artyhearts either. Poon popped up one day. A quick, chatty mail from Koh Samui where she was on holiday after her monastery expedition. Milly was in Australia—Ms Eternal Wanderer could not stay put if she tried. No mails from her. I wrote to Poon telling her everything that had happened. Didn't hear back, but she had said that she was going to be offline for the most part until she was back in Bangkok. I wrote to Andrew a couple of times but not a peep from him.

I went out every night with the girls, determined not to sit next to my computer. I even went to some office shindig—something I'd have never, never done if I wasn't in such a daze. On New Year's, I met a college boyfriend and we made out a bit.

After another week, I totally flipped. I looked up Andrew's official email address on his website and wrote there. After two days, I got a polite email from, I think, his secretary. 'Mr Wylie is afraid you may have the wrong address.' I wrote to her explaining a little more about the Bob Dylan project without mentioning the website I had met kinky Mr Wylie on. She wrote back again. 'Mr Wylie says he is afraid no longer since he has no idea what you are talking about.' A few mails back and forth later, she wrote back again. A bitchy mail. 'I regretfully must suggest to you that you have been taken in by a case of identity theft. An Andrew Wiley impersonator.'

12 January. 9 a.m.

I read her mail and felt sick to my stomach. I called work and told them I wasn't coming in. They could go fuck themselves. I told my mother I had a migraine and got into bed. I put a pillow over my head. How had this happened?

I tried to retrace my steps. Andrew had found me. No. Milly had introduced me to him online. Her old friend from New York. I jumped out of bed. I sent Milly a very formal mail asking her how well she knew Andrew because there had been an incident I wanted to discuss.

A whole day passed. Nothing.

I went to work and mailed Milly again. Ccing Poon, begging them to respond. Nothing for days. I found Milly's official email address on her blog and mailed her there. I got an automated response: Hi. I'm at an artists' residency in Japan from August 2008 to March 2009. I apologise if I don't get back to you right away because I have decided to spend very little time online. Must give the writing a fighting chance! Hope you will understand.

August 2008 to March 2009 in Japan. But Milly had been in Singapore and Australia and online talking to me all day all that time. Unless, of course, Milly was a fake too. Fuck my life. In a rage, I wrote to Poon, asking what on earth was going on. Who were all these frauds she had introduced me to? Was she a fake too? I half-hoped for an angry response from her explaining that this was all some big mess-up. Someone had hacked into someone's artyhearts account. Something of that sort.

Of course, I never heard back from her again.

Over the week, I thought of how I'd been handed from fraud to fraud to fraud till I was totally ripped off.

Then it occurred to me that perhaps they were all one person. One person slowly pulling this con on an innocent Indian woman. Taking advantage of my pro-activeness and initiative and can-do spirit.

My head hurt to think of all the work involved in creating such an elaborate con. Hours of chatting. Back stories. Locations. Photos were easy for Milly and Andrew since they were actual people whose pictures were online. I didn't think Poon was a real person. Anyway, she knew too much about India for a Thai photographer who has been to India a couple of times. Her pictures must be from stock photos of some girl somewhere.

What I didn't get was this. Why me? What had they hoped for? Had there been a money angle? I thought about that for a while. No. That didn't make sense because they had stopped corresponding as soon as I sent in the songs for Bob Dylan.

Were they hoping to publish my songs under some other name? No. Too much work. And anyway it wasn't 'they'. If it was one person, which it must be, then who was it? Could it be Manav? I had told him to fuck off and he was a techie. Who could write. Sort of.

I read all the chats, all the emails and kept looking for clues. I think the last straw was when I had realised that Milly had even made up artists and books. That Thai poetry book about a dhobi or whatever she'd recommended to me was totally made-up shit. I kinda hated artyhearts after that and never went back.

After a week, I calmed down a bit. Luckily, I had not told anyone. Except Cyrus, whom I had not talked to since he laughed at me, no one knew that I had been conned like a halli-gugu.

Back to the old life. Drinking with the girls. Girls minus Mrs Anita who was still a prisoner to the babies and Prakash. I wondered whether she was stuck with them forever, since her brother was showing no signs of wanting them back. The thought reminded me that I hadn't seen her in ages. I called. She told me to come for dinner.

I got there in a bad mood. I stomped into her house after fighting with an auto-driver. My mood didn't get better. The babies now had an ayah, but Anita was in some crazy house-cleaning mood. So I had to sit around feeling murderous and bored while she scrubbed everything, including the buckets in the bathroom. Luckily, I had bought a nice copy of the complete Sherlock Holmes from one of those guys who sold books at traffic lights, so I pulled it out of my bag and began reading. I love Sherlock Holmes. Every single story. I had read the whole set when I got the measles. Then again when I got chicken pox and jaundice, but I hadn't read it in years.

As soon as I began re-reading A *Case of Identity*, I knew how and who had conned me. You must have read Holmes when you were a kid, but you may not remember this story. So basically, there is this girl called Mary who comes to see Sherlock Holmes. She was engaged to a guy who had disappeared without a trace at the church just before their wedding ceremony. When Sherlock finds him, he finds out the mysterious lover was actually Mary's youngish stepfather who had seduced her. In disguise. He did it to ensure that Mary would always pine for her lost fiancé and never get married. So that he would always have access to her money.

I knew the person who had conned me had to be Prakash! He was trying to teach me a lesson. Get me off internet dating forever by screwing me over. All those different countries and identities, he could have done it with his hands tied behind his back, the fucking nerd.

I wanted to kill him. I thought of ways to kill him as Anita and I ate mountains of bisi bele bath slouched on her huge American couch. I barely said a word. Luckily, having seen me through my worst years and rants and rages, Anita didn't mind my mood. At some point, I wanted to slap her also for marrying Prakash. So, I really didn't have anything to say.

We were sitting around drinking coffee when Prakash arrived. He was his usual Rainman self. White shirt clean. Pants uncreased. Neat as hell even though it was the middle of the night. Wide eyes and spiky eyelashes behind his spectacles. Mumbling things under the breath. I watched him clean up the kitchen and settle Anita's baby nieces into their cot. For a minute I was convinced I had got it all wrong.

Prakash joined us at the table with his coffee. We were silent for a few minutes. Then he asked, 'How is your internet dating going?' My tongue felt thick and huge in my mouth. I wanted to knock him down from the sofa and jump up and down on his chest with my heels. I was about to snarl at him when, from the corner of my eye, I saw a strange smirk pass over Anita's face. I looked again and it was gone. I said something random to Prakash and watched her face. There it was. A fit of giggles she was trying to hide in her cup of coffee.

All this time, while I was thinking it was Prakash, it was okay...sort of. But for it to be Anita? It had to be her. Prakash did not have the fucking imagination for such a con. I wanted to strangle her. Anita had patiently waited and pushed me off a cliff for no reason. What had I ever done to her? I looked at her, determined to have it out in the open now. Fuck the friendship.

I opened my mouth. Then she looked up from her coffee and at me, with a face as smooth as chocolate. Just those big, terrifying eyes daring me to say something, anything.

I said nothing. Perhaps these were the first signs that I was going mad. Maybe this is what happens if you are twenty-seven and unmarried. You start imagining things.

The Triangle

This was her only romantic fantasy. One in which the man she is in love with becomes incandescent with jealousy because of a man who was in love with her. This was her only fantasy so she frugally squeezed infinite versions out of it. So many versions it should have been the same old dal, but it remained sweet and creamy.

ONE

She is staring at the checkerboard floor of the bar smiling gently and her lover is smiling at her. His is a beautiful smile with a clear varnish of smugness, a smile in full possession of the knowledge that she is in his thrall. He is a beautiful man, so it is easy to ignore the radiance of his sureness. Or it should be easy, but she is finding it hard. Everything is hard with this one. She keeps her bra on when she is on top as if that will shield her from her unsureness, as if it will steady her rhythm with him. Then she sleeps with her clothes off because under the sheets in the dark, she is as smooth and unblemished as she would wish to be with him.

Unable to be less in love with him, she has decided it is easier if she is also in love with someone else.

Someone else. It could be someone brand new, but really where is the fun in someone brand new? What would be better than the man with whom she has most deployed 'it's complicated'? Let him descend the staircase from the afternoon stillness of the first floor of the bar onto the checkerboard. Let him almost leave before he sees her. He is not so beautiful. He is as beautiful as she is, just beautiful enough to feel like they have, as the song goes, game by the pound. He almost leaves and then sees her from the corner of his eye, holding hands with a good-looking stranger. He pivots and greets her warmly. Introductions abound. The two men chat. This is the part of the fantasy she dislikes the most, but she hasn't found a way of making the transition to the next stage with any other filler. Surely the waiter cannot drop a tray before introductions are made. If the tray is dropped too far from them, they wouldn't care. If the tray is dropped too close to them, her lover is either likely to say something to the waiter and either damn himself or requite himself with his grasp on their class dynamic. Either way, this would tilt the balance dramatically. She doesn't want to pick one or the other lover. She wants them to pick her. So, introductions have to be made.

Her complication leaves the table smoothly after a brief conversation, but then circles back to ask to speak to her in private. The complication has a dense, dark, powerful upper body and a dense, dark beard. She knows from intimate experience that the old-god body rested on surprisingly thin legs and that his power was fuelled by rage. He draws her to a quiet corner of the checkerboard. A wall of fire explodes between them and over the flames he rages at her. He summons up an ethical argument for being angry that she is with this new golden lover. She is scornful of his moral outrage and tells him straight: you are a dog in the manger. His forehead registers a tsunami of frowns. She is delusional, he signals, but she stands her ground. She lists the occasions he has wanted her—all the times some other man wanted her. He looks like he is going to laugh in disbelief. She reaches her hands above the wall of fire and takes his hands. He is perfectly capable of shaking her hands off, being a wholesale rager and a wholesale fake-rejecter of sentimentality. She stands her ground and holds his hands. You will always be my darling complication. Always, darling.

She turns around and glides smoothly across the checkerboard stage in her black tulle skirt, glides across to her lover who is in position for her grand jeté. She never worries about him not catching her when she leaps.

She doesn't look back at the complication because his hurt would make her hurt and lose her lines in this karmically and aesthetically appropriate exit.

This version makes her cry and also gives her an orgasm. Always.

TWO

Some afternoons she can't make the two men disaggregate their conversation and display of manliness. The men talk to each other and laugh and show their strong, white teeth. On one occasion, when she didn't keep even her modest control on the reins of the fantasy, the scene dissolved so badly she avoided her blanket cave for anything other than sleep for many months. That time, the golden boy expressed his admiration for the complication's manly, hairy chest visible at the top of his soft, cotton shirt. They laugh. She just sits at the table with a fixed, benign expression, like a woman in a Mahesh Elkunchwar play.

It's hard to get the rhythm and pressure right, but once you do, and you know what works best for you, then you can build castles and dig rivers and make whole landscapes behind your eyes as your fingers work away. It's an MMORPG for one. It's an orgy for one. Oh gee. Oh ji. Oh oh oh.

THREE

She swiped right on the complication. Quick, heated texts lead to a demand that they meet that evening in a hotel. It seems a bit rich for her blood even if he is the proverbial dark, handsome stranger, so she never replies. Perhaps his confidence is a bit rich for her blood. She thinks of him and tastes marrow and fat on her tongue.

Another one glows gold in her phone screen and his charm is malai. He invites her for drinks at a bar with a checkerboard floor, making jokes about who can afford what. Afterwards, they are holding hands and they drift out of the bar together through a tree-lined street to the same hotel the app boy had wanted to meet in. She had seen the drift many streets ago but did nothing to stop it. When they check in, she easily arranges her face into one that checks into hotels all the time for a golden romp. All the time, darling. He is holding her hand with his right hand, and signing things and filling things with his left one. She wonders if there is a right-handed version of him living on the other side of the large, curvaceous mirror in the lobby.

Tethered firmly, she turns back and forth. She does the shimmy and the jitterbug. Then she sees him. Dark, dense body. Thick lashes whipping accusations at her. His lower lip is full and is a few grams short of a sulk.

In the bubble elevator, as they swish up, she can't resist draping herself across the new lover like a girl in a James Bond poster. He looks up from his left-hand phone to smile absently at her. On their floor, she sneaks a look over the railings at the lobby below. The thunderous, tsunami brow of her complication is visible even from this height.

Sex is golden and she arises smoothly, leaving him smiling and smooth-chested in bed.

In the lobby, she stops for a coffee and strokes the inner wrist of the waiter, startling herself and the waiter. Her complication is still here. He looks up from his armchair, angry and scornful. She has confirmed his worst prejudices and can't take his eyes off her. Her coffee is excellent.

When she is able to focus and tune the fantasy with attention and care, like the conductor of an orchestra, this one gives her hours of pleasure.

FOUR

He glowers, golden and rendered interesting because of the bitterness slowly twisting his lips. He is at the far end of the garden.

The flowers sometimes escape her control and grow house-size, making the cast teeny-tiny. But they are always tulip red, even if they are not tulips. Sometimes they are hibiscuses, trumpety and trailing tendrils.

She and the complication are laughing. They are leaning into each other in a way that always makes her think of Sandra Bullock, who is accused of leaning in *While You Were Sleeping*. It's not hugging, but it is sexy because they are pretending to hug and daring anyone to say otherwise. *We stand just a little too close, we stare just a little too long.* Leaning is such a hot activity, it makes Bill Pullman hottish.

The complication has eyes like searchlights, always scanning for weakness and cracks in the varnish. Except when they lean into each other. He relaxes then. Then they rest like conjoined twins, resigned, relieved and unable to imagine a universe in which they are not voices to voices, lip to lip, dirty hip to hip.

Just for a second, she rests her head on his chest. Just for a second, he rests his head on her shoulder.

FIVE

In the checkerboard garden, the hibiscuses and tulips have grown horse high. She fights her way through to the clearing in her green chiffon sari that slips off frequently. She reaches the narrow night watchman's box. She steps in to fix her sari. She stands there waiting for the dream production to drape her sari better. Occasionally, she looks down to check the progress on the pleats. She looks up and to see that both of them, her lover and the complication, have made it past the flowers and into the clearing. They stare at her standing straight in the box. The green chiffon shimmers and slithers. Even on her most slack, disinterested days, the sari never falls. A girl has her pride.

SIX

Sometimes she freezes the scene so she can slide from chair to chair, from lap to lap to stroke their cheeks, look in their eyes, lick their upper lips with her stiffened tongue. Once, the golden one cried for her. He cried beautifully. She paused the scene to lick the salt path across the desert of his cheeks. She twisted in his lap, to look over her shoulder at her complication in the other chair. He was stilled in a moment of mischief and superiority. Like he'd rather die than cry. Like he could take it or leave it. Like he could take her or leave her, as he always has. Who weeps? In the warm, golden lap, holding on to warm, golden shoulders, she looks back and forth.

Catchin' feelings is a no, sang the man. But in the blanket cave, she wants to eat the feelings. She eats them all up very slowly.

Mindful

Her husband's hair was largely the source of his happiness and, as Rhea was beginning to realise, the source of her dissatisfaction. Though he was thirty-six, Mathew's thick hair conveyed a youthful air of irrepressibleness. Combined with the enormous warmth he turned on as soon as he left their home, it was no surprise to anyone that Mathew was a success at work. Only Rhea found it hard to compose her face whenever she had to respond appropriately to his fans. She bumped into his admirers among strangers, his large family and the hordes of her own family she was still discovering in the three years since they'd moved from Delhi to Ernakulam.

Rhea looked up grumpily from her pillow to figure out what he was saying. It was close to midnight and they had been lying side-by-side for a couple hours, but she had forgotten that he was in the room.

She took her headphones out and, distracted by the inky sheen and volume of his hair, failed to understand his intentions. 'I've got rid of all the junk apps and my phone is so fast now. Here, give me yours.' Mathew tried to prise the phone out of her hand. She wanted to punch him. When he looked surprised at her resistance, she gave in and he was soon trawling through her apps, laughing and uninstalling. 'Oho, two different apps to remind you to drink water. Why don't you just drink water when you are thirsty? Three different apps to track your periods, Rhea, man.' She closed her eyes, took a deep breath and took her phone back.

'I will delete them.'

'You should! Start the new year with a clean inbox and clean phone. You can certainly delete that meditation app. I don't think I have ever seen you use it.'

Rhea grunted and turned her back to him, put her headphones back on and closed her eyes. A friend visiting from Delhi had recommended Chill. Nayantara had lain on Rhea's couch, raving about it. Nayantara was perfect from her pale pink toenails to her blue-dipped hair. Rhea had subscribed to Chill while Nayantara was still mid-rave about the calm the app had bought to her life. Then she had forgotten all about it.

In the way that he occasionally did, and almost always in matters of money, Mathew became fixated on the meditation app.

The next morning. 'It's called Chill but it costs Rs 4,000 a year. That's not so chill, alle?' Rhea didn't disagree. Since they had moved to Ernakulam, she had lost her life, her friends and the ease of her quasi-mother-tongue Hindi, but all that would have been bearable if

Mathew wasn't suddenly earning three times what she earned. They now rarely thought for two minutes before buying anything, but if ever they did, it was when Mathew commented about something she had bought in her admittedly thoughtless way.

After work that evening, when Rhea was soaking dried fruit and nuts in rum and looking up her mother's Christmas-cake recipe, she remembered that conversation about the app and was annoyed afresh. When did she ever ask him what he was spending his money on? She ground her teeth, caught herself at it and stuffed a great handful of the chopped apricots in her mouth. She wiped her hands on her jeans. Then she thought, as she did at least once a day, that Mathew would never do such a thing. Her parents admired how neat he was and occasionally sighed regretfully that she still wasn't.

She switched from the recipe back to her Korean show and was about to prop her phone against the maida dabba when she got a notification from Chill. 'Coping with self-esteem issues with trips to the fridge?' She was startled and amused. Algorithms had got cute. So cute that she could imagine the phone had heard her grind her teeth and gulp down those rummy apricots. I Spy with My Digital Eye.

She clicked on the notification and a sweet little pastel animated fridge offered to talk her out of emotional eating.

'Hello, Chill, got ESP?' The sound of her own voice didn't startle her anymore. She had become a full-fledged talker to self in their fifteenth-floor apartment. Mathew loved to tell his friends back home that even the mosquitoes took the lift to their flat. She felt much more cut-off here than in their crumbling, ridiculously expensive Delhi rental which didn't even have the 'fa' of 'facilities'.

She abandoned the cake prep and wandered into her beautiful sea-green living room. All their visitors looked at her messy, frizzy hair, looked at the living room and immediately complimented Mathew for it. Surely it must be his elegant eye that created this soothing beauty.

Rhea sat down and put on her headphones to try the guided meditation the cartoon fridge had offered. She was startled by the pure gold of the man's voice in her ears. She sat up. 'Gently close your eyes. Allow your mind to wander like a puppy. Watch it, don't scold it. In time we will teach the puppy to sit down. We will teach the puppy to sit again and again, but today is not that day.'

The voice in her ear reminded her of one perfect winter afternoon when she and a college friend had lay about in Lodhi gardens. They had been slightly drunk and the grass slightly damp, but they had sunglasses on and several layers of shawls. Rhea remembered feeling like she would have been quite content to die that moment. Today is not that day.

Three nights later, she half-watched Mathew pack for a trip to Prague to hang out with one of his big paprika vendors. The spice company his school friend had founded frequently sent Mathew abroad. Tonight she felt less annoyed with him than usual, even when he was sending her all over the house to find him things, even when he was continuously reciting stages of his travel plans. She was four sessions down on the app's Peace and Quiet meditation series. She was breathing differently, she noticed. It was slower, more measured. She sat quietly while Mathew bustled about and then saw the notification on her phone. Chill was saying: we are proud of you, aren't you proud of you?

As soon as Mathew was out of the door, she put on her headphones and lay on the planter's chair in their balcony. She had looked up the owner of that golden voice after two sessions.

On Tuesday, she had looked at Kabir's photos on Instagram and felt lit from within by the kindness in his eyes, his lean, otherworldly body.

On Wednesday, she considered giving up meat. Rhea also felt disproportionately upset at the number of women commenting on his photos. And she felt upset thinking about it now. She picked a module on honesty, adjusted the volume and prepared to drown in Kabir's voice. One hand scrabbled about her purse for a cigarette.

The next Saturday, Mathew was home. He took a sudden detour from a lecture about their mutual funds to ask whether she had cancelled all her subscriptions. 'You don't need three music streaming apps, Rhea, do you? These little things add up.'

In the afternoon, she deleted two music apps and immediately regretted it. It was as if most of the ropes tying her balloon to the ground had been cut off. She looked at Mathew, adjusting the angle of their ceiling-mounted projector to watch IPL and wondered whether their lives were wholly imaginary. Perhaps he was imaginary. Perhaps Kabir was imaginary too. An AI fantasy on an AI beach. All was imaginary except for that voice in her ear. Now that she had personalised the settings on the app, Kabir's voice whispered her name in her ear. Close your eyes, Rhea. Scan your body, Rhea. Begin at your toes, Rhea.

Mathew was saying something, but Rhea pretended not to have heard. She picked up her phone. A notification from Chill had popped up just below a notification about a good deal on biryani.

'People are not what they seem to be, Rhea.'

Kabir was beginning to sound like a newspaper horoscope, Rhea thought to herself in mild irritation.

A new notification popped up. 'Running out of empathy, Rhea?' On her sea-green sofa, she jumped. This was a bit too much. She stuffed her phone under a cushion and went for a walk. But without her usual music playing overly loud in her ears, she found herself unexpectedly accompanied by the choir of competing voices in her head. Rhea hated them. She should have brought her phone and Kabir along.

When she came back, Mathew was watching IPL. She smelt the new pink pepper sample he had brought home the previous evening.

She breathed in the pepper and immediately imagined herself gliding in the long green dress Keira Knightley had worn in *Atonement*. Why that dress? It came to her in a dizzying flash. File retrieval had sped up in these post-Chill days. She had once taken a personality test run by a perfumier and the test had dazzled her by identifying a perfect perfume for her—one with pink peppers in it. The perfumier and she had gone to watch *Atonement* together in Delhi.

A second string of memories. She remembered that fancy French perfume had a Pondicherry connection. From Instagram, she knew Kabir lived in Pondicherry.

She stuffed her running shoes into the shelf, dropped her socks in the laundry bag and was astounded by a new stack of stray thoughts. She heard one of her voices scheming a girls' trip to Pondicherry only so she could bump into Kabir.

Watch the puppy? The puppy was totally out of control! She fished the phone out from under the cushion and went to the settings to uninstall the damn app once and for all.

A new notification. 'Aren't you impressed by how the universe is responding to your needs? We are impressed.' She stared at her phone.

Another notification. 'Fix your head and you can fix your hair later.'

She put her headphones on to listen.

All Girls Together

Girls had changed. Girls had changed too much, Sheela felt.

Sheela had only been away four years, but when she was around her team, it felt like she had arrived from the 1940s in a khadi sari. She had been prepared to be cheerful, to be a good boss, to be the exact opposite of the bosses she had had. Sheela had planned to be understanding. She was going to take the girls out for a drink once in a while, to be available if they had any personal problems. But somewhere between 2014 and 2018, while she had been at home with her daughter, girls had stopped smiling or laughing at jokes. They only stared at her when she said something funny.

They didn't like being called girls either, she had recently discovered. One of them, Sheela didn't know which one, had printed a meme and left it on her desk. Some actress saying, 'Don't call me girl, sir!' Sheela didn't recognise the actress and it bothered her. So, she spent some time at home reverse-searching until she found her. She had definitely never seen a movie with this one in it. Sheela was careful to never call her colleagues girls again, but it felt like a loss the first few times she censored herself. She remembered her college friend Liz, small and bouncy, standing in the aisle of the excursion bus they took from Bangalore to Goa, saying Girls, Girls, Girls each time she had some new dumb joke or announcement. Girls, girls, girls, I have a very serious announcement, she'd say and then start laughing. Come on, girls, don't laugh. Come on, girls.

Sheela didn't need this drama at the beginning of a brand-new project the whole world was talking about. It was a lot of pressure. Especially since the whole world actually was talking about it in the media, but she and the team could not discuss it with anyone. They had all signed non-disclosure agreements two weeks before the announcement. Of course, her team complained about how many times they had to sign. They came in from legal, laughing and rubbing their arms as if they had been doing manual labour. That was a few days before they were told the details of the actual work. And that was when her job really became stressful.

Sheela, a woman whose boyfriends had always called her no-nonsense, thought it was a great idea. Men were pigs and were constantly putting naked pictures of their girlfriends or ex-girlfriends online to punish them. Can you stop men from being pigs? No. So why not try out the solution the company had come up with. 'Our motto is to make an impact. So if you don't want to be part of the solution, you just want to be part of the problem,' she told the girls. She could see Mansi and a couple others rolling their eyes, but she saw two of her team nodding thoughtfully. Women's safety was an issue that was on everyone's mind after all.

On the bus home, she couldn't stop obsessing. They passed a new children's soft play centre with huge plate glass windows. Stuck in traffic she watched kids squeezing through tunnels and hurtling down slides for nearly half an hour. It struck her that part of the misery came from the space her team shared. The team had been pulled off the main floor and into one of the small, glass-walled conference rooms to work in privacy. What privacy. Sure, everyone couldn't see your nose-hairs the way they usually could on the main floors. For the world's biggest social media company, they were pretty kanjoos about space. And as a manager it would have been nice for her to not be practically sitting on the laps of her direct reports. But in the conference room, the six of them were stuck with just each other and this difficult pilot project. The girls weren't chatterboxes. That wasn't the problem. In fact, it was the opposite—a permanently tense silence, as if she had screwed up or was about to. Occasionally, two of them would start laughing, making it clear to everyone else that they had been chatting online. The others never asked 'tell us the joke also'. Sheela did once, right at the beginning but her good humour evaporated when they only stared at her silently, unwilling to part with whatever gem they had shared with each other.

That was on the inside. On the outside, the whole floor was staring at them like they were fish in an aquarium. They couldn't talk about it and didn't. But when the first announcements went out about the anti-revenge-porn project, people on the outside pieced together enough to understand that Sheela and her team were in charge of looking at naked women all day. The speed with which they pieced this together from the 1,600 internal emails that flooded their inbox every day amazed Sheela. She opened her inbox a million times a day, still terrified she'd miss something crucial. And sometimes did. But some people replied to everything and some people were quick to follow the sequence of events that led to Sheela and the girls being stuck in the aquarium.

The company had taken a big decision and needed to persuade its millions of daily active users to come on board. If men were going to violate the privacy of women, why not take some insurance? You fill a form and then you upload your photos yourself to a private database using an encrypted link that the company gave you.

She had asked at their first two-day training session about the responsible storage of these images. The reply from the International Head of Safety in Mountain View had reassured her. Bow (short for Rainbow) had leant earnestly into the screen, 'No, we won't be storing these images. We will generate a digital image hash.'

Mansi asked with her best old Western movie cowboy accent: A who?

Sheela turned to glare, but Bow laughed. 'It's a unique code. It's the kind of thing that lets us do reverse-image search on Google, for instance. So the photo has a code. Then, if a bad-faith actor uploads a copy of the same photo, we can match the photo against the code and block the copies from circulation.'

An hour later, she was squeezed, standing between Vineeta and Mansi's chairs, helping Vineeta with a process, feeling unhappily aware of Mansi's judgey-judgey body next to her. Through a series of surreptitious eye movements, she saw Mansi Whatsapping Karunya.

Knock, knock.

Why did you break up with your crazy ex-boyfriend?

Because he was a bad-faith actor.

Karunya sent her a gif of a woman spitting up her drink.

Completely blank expressions as they were doing all this, of course. Sheela nearly sighed out loud but controlled herself. Back in her first stint at the company, she had gone through bootcamp and so many training sessions and always had such a good time. They had all been so enthu, not like this permanently negative lot. She really would have to work hard to keep them on track.

She didn't want to be so depressed before it even started. It was a big responsibility. And there was a reason why they had been picked. 'Because white people want us to do their dirty work, but they think Indian men are too dirty to be trusted with naked photos. That's why brown girls get to do this job,' said Mansi. That girl's eyes were going to get stuck permanently looking upwards, like one of her daughter Aaliya's old dolls. Mansi made the others feel bad if they were positive about anything. Sheela wanted to tell Mansi that if you were the colour of maida, you didn't get to call yourself a brown girl. If only there was a way of sending her to Gurgaon. But no, Mansi was a local and not only called herself brown, she also called herself ex-North Indian and insisted on eating beef for every meal.

Willy from Bow's team had flown in for the dry run. Even though she had braced herself, Sheela couldn't stop the thud of shock at looking at a series of naked and near-naked bodies on a Monday morning at work. Plus the whole office was probably trying to peer into the aquarium to see what was on their screens. She couldn't look to see if they were looking. Because then her team would know that she was scared and embarrassed. They were looking at her for her reaction even though they pretended they weren't. That much she knew for sure. Willy, a tall, tattoo-sleeved woman, watched her patiently as she learnt to review photos and 'hash' them. 'Good job, Sheela. Now the rest of you get started on your folders, and Sheela and I can help you with anything that gives you pause,' she said.

For a while, they all worked silently, only occasionally looking at the whiteboard, which had words to remind them in case they forgot what would be considered offensive. Did anyone really need the list? When you saw a woman's private parts with a phone stuck in it, did you really need a reminder?

But after a few hours, Sheela had to admit that women's bodies were so strangely shaped that it took quite a bit of expertise to identify body parts. She was feeling a bit like the blind men and the elephant each time she looked at one. Was it a vagina? Or was it a piece of plastic?

What would she have done if she had known what she was getting into? The job description had said 'Head, Community Standards Operations (Special Division)' and the job couldn't have come at a better time. Aaliya was at school half the day and Sheela was keen to get back before she became officially unemployable. Four years was a long time away, so she was surprised that she had been hired so speedily and without too many snide comments. Everyone had said it would be hard to get back in the game. None of her old colleagues (except Manu) were around, but she had solid experience in Community Management, so that must have counted.

When the dry runs were done and they were ready to get started, Sheela knew it was time to completely give up on her vision of this new job and what kind of boss she would be. She couldn't hope to have the kind of simple life where she would look up from a photo, catch the eye of her colleagues and have a shared giggle of embarrassment at their bizarre new job. No chance she would be able to throw her hands in the air and say, yaar, what kind of couple wants to take pictures like these? There was no hope of being girls together.

Not that Mansi didn't like to joke with Willy. Mid-morning, on their second day in the silent conference room, Sheela heard Mansi say, 'oh, hello, pussy'. She turned her head sharply and found Mansi and Willy laughing a little at the photo of a naked woman lying in bed with a cat between her thighs. The cat was staring into the camera and the spread-eagled woman was not. 'This is a tough one, team,' said Willy composing her face back into its usual impassive half smile. 'Sure, Willy,' said Mansi rolling her big eyes and smiling. Sheela felt a jolt. Then a second jolt. First, because that was a flirty eye-roll if she had ever seen one. And then the realisation that she felt jealous. Jealous of what? Hash it, hash it, hash it.

Every time she saw a nipple she wondered whether it was a message. Not from God, not from Him. But every time she saw a nipple, it felt like a Whatsapp message she didn't want to open but she could see the top line. The squirmy hot pressure between her thighs every single time couldn't be wholly ignored. But she had successfully ignored it for two weeks. She was afraid that her team would notice.

At mid-day, Reema burst into tears and startled the rest of them. When they looked at her screen, they all felt ready to join her. A naked woman, like hundreds they had seen before. But this one was blindfolded and in tears. Almost certainly the smears on her arms and chest were blood. Sheela took over and encouraged the others to take Reema to coffee. When she finished, she joined them in the canteen, but no one wanted to speak.

Tomorrow was Saturday and they wouldn't have to look at any nudes and on Sunday was her niece's first Holy Communion party and, with luck, she wouldn't think of nipples then. But for a month that was all Sheela had looked at all day and nipples flew through her dreams like strangely shaped birds.

Eager to be home, she took a cab and fell asleep. Sheela was shocked when she woke up nearly an hour later and close to home. She was never so casual about her safety. But she was feeling ill. She saw the big, red-rimmed, round mirror that always comforted her — a simple, pretty solution to a dangerous blind corner in her neighbourhood. Tonight, though, she blinked because it brought back her dream in living colour.

She had dreamt she was in an American-style white wedding gown. No, just the veil and shoes and she was naked. She was sitting on the lap of a burly man and he was sucking hard at her nipple. His mouth and teeth made her left nipple hurt. Her hands were clenching the man's thighs. Clawing at his black trousers, she twisted sideways to give him more and she looked into the eyes of the burly man and saw herself. Himself. She was sucking at the breast of a woman, naked except for a wedding veil and shoes. He was. Dreams are so rubbish. As rubbish as people who are stupid enough to let their boyfriends take their naked pictures. As if they didn't know what happens these days.

On Sunday evening, the after-communion party had run on for many hours after the grandparents left. The adults were seeing each other after a long while. And they were all dressed up. It was not surprising that someone had put on dance music. They liked to have a good time, her siblings and her husband's siblings. Usually she had a great time dancing, but somehow she just couldn't feel the music. The younger people were playing DJ and she didn't recognise too many of the songs. She felt ready to cry. And then her husband put on one of their old favourites, *Senorita* from *Zindagi Na Milegi Dobara*. It always made them feel romantic and they danced close. Someone dimmed the lights. She inhaled the familiar smell of her husband's chest and smiled to herself. Just as she was feeling like herself, her happy sensible self, just as she remembered she was one half of a couple the whole family envied, she heard a solitary giggle. She turned around and saw that everyone else had stopped dancing and were all watching her youngest sister-in-law doing a parody flamenco, flailing and throwing her legs about dramatically with her eyes closed. Making fun of her. She was too depressed to be angry with the attention-seeking bitch. She forced herself to smile a little and went to the kitchen to drink water.

On Monday, she decided to go have coffee with Manu, hoping that talking to someone outside the aquarium would help her mood. Manu was also back in the company after a couple years away and he definitely had something to do with her being hired, she had thought.

Back in the day, she and Manu had never been close friends, but she believed that he thought of her as a reliable no-nonsense type. Which she was. At least she used to be. Whenever she looked around, everyone in her team was working. Headphones on, ordering lunch, browsing Instagram occasionally but mostly working. She was the only one getting psyched by looking at naked bodies all day.

Manu complained to her about the young people he was working with and the company's work culture. 'I had forgotten how stupid the decision-making process is. How is it that interns get to decide policy? Just because the bosses want to feel young,' he said. Sheela remembered that she had liked Manu for this, for thinking about the big picture at work even when they were very young. But perhaps he was fed up with his own complaining because in a bit he dropped the bitterness and told her a series of comical stories about his team.

'Why are they always carrying water bottles, Sheela? From one desk to the next? It's not like we are working in a construction site.' She laughed and for a moment her heart was lighter. Then she noticed that his pants were narrower and tighter than they used to be. And remembered that she was almost certain she saw him wearing boots the previous week. Boots! In Bangalore! And in a flash she imagined Manu naked except for boots. She closed her eyes hard, like someone pulling down the shutter of the shop for the day. She mumbled something to quiet the porn film in her head. Manu asked her what she was saying and she couldn't say anything light or normal enough. They left the canteen soon after. Back in the office, nothing was better. She couldn't get rid of the naked Instagram filter installed in her head.

When the breaking point came though, she was far away from the office, hurtling down the road on the pillion of a scooter.

On Thursday, she reviewed a set of images that seemed to have been shot in an office. The photos seemed so posed that Reema showed it to her wondering if they were stills from a movie. Even if they were, they had no place on the site, she said to Reema. But they weren't. Someone somewhere not in a film studio had taken this one.

In the photo, the three women were topless, sitting on a couch and holding cushions on their laps. All three cushions had the same message printed on them: 'Comfy?' Hash them, she told Reema.

But Reema's computer hung and it took ten whole minutes before the photo left Sheela's line of vision. The mid-afternoon slump was making her eyes close. For a second, she drifted into sleep and shook herself awake. She stood up firmly and her head swam a little. She sat down abruptly again. She closed her eyes and all she could see were the three women holding the 'Comfy?' cushions and their three sets of surprisingly matched breasts. Except for the colour of the nipples. Those were different. One woman had cherry-coloured nipples. What would they taste like? Sheela stood up abruptly again and left the aquarium for a walk.

The next evening, she was outside waiting for the office cab when Mansi appeared on her scooter and offered her a lift. She didn't quite fancy the long, uncomfortable ride back on a two-wheeler, but in the interests of getting along, she said yes, sounding extravagantly grateful. She hoped she hadn't forgotten the knack of riding pillion and swung her leg over. Mansi turned to her and asked, 'Comfy?' Sheela felt her thighs clench together near painfully in arousal. Through the helmet's clear visor, she saw Mansi's beautiful eyes first widen and then crinkle in amusement. Mansi didn't say anything, but all the way home, Sheela wondered what exactly to say in the email demanding a transfer out of the aquarium and its bodies.

Acknowledgements

Thank you, Gaurav Jain, my husband and pal in all kinds of risky business. As a writer if you must marry, then it is wise to marry a stylish writer and editor. As a writer if you must marry, then it is wise to marry Gaurav Jain.

Thanks to my parents T.A. Abraham and Annamma Abraham, for teaching me to read, write and make PJs in two languages and tolerating me in others.

Thanks to Paromita Vohra, whose marvellous mind and voice at the other end of the phone line has enlivened my life for a decade. She is the *OG* My Brilliant Friend.

Thanks to my friend Jugal Mody who cannot help making art and being loving in all his waking hours.

Thanks to my friend Avinash Kuduvalli who is always ready for a new adventure and who is tolerant of the unadventurous.

Thanks to my friend and agent Jayapriya Vasudevan for moving the mountains needed to make literary careers possible and for teaching me how to keep infants occupied.

Thanks to my friend Meera Pillai who appreciates the effort of snark and the effort of resisting snark equally.

Thanks to my editors Karthika V.K. and Ajitha G.S., unmatched in their meticulous, genial and enthusiastic dealings with writers. Thank you for making everything seem fun, possible and within reach.

Copyright Acknowledgements

'The Women Who Forgot to Invent Facebook' was first published in the March 2012 issue of *Out of Print* magazine.

'The Trinity' was first published, in a slightly different version, in November 2013 in *n+1* magazine's online edition.

'Teresa' was first published, in a slightly different version, in the 1 August 2013 issue of *The Caravan*.

'The Gentle Reader' was first published, in a slightly different version, in January 2013 in *Pratilipi* magazine.

'The Singer and the Prince' was first published, in a slightly different version, in April 2013 in *n+1* magazine's online edition.

'Missed Call' was first published, in a slightly different version, in the anthology *Of Mothers and Others*, edited by Jaishree Misra, Zubaan, 2013.

'Mindful' was first published, in a slightly different version, in the 29 December 2019 issue of *The Indian Express*'s *Eye* magazine.